JOE WILLIS

WRITTEN BY
JOEL N. CAMPBELL

First published in paperback in 2025
by 104 Books

© Joel N. Campbell 2025

Joel N. Campbell asserts the moral right to be identified as the author of this work.

All rights reserved. No part of this publication may be reproduced, stored in a retrieval system or transmitted, in any form or by any means, electronic, mechanical, photocopying, recording and/or otherwise without the prior written permission of the publishers. This book may not be lent, resold, hired out or disposed of by way of trade in any form, binding or cover other than that in which it is published without the prior written consent of the publishers.

This is a work of fiction. Names, characters, businesses, places, events and incidents are either the products of the author's imagination or used in a fictitious manner. Any resemblance to actual persons, living or dead, or actual events and places is purely coincidental.

CONTENTS

Acknowledgements..ii
Preface..v
About The Author..ix
Aberdare Encounter..1
Recruiting the 'Special One'...5
We meet again...7
What's the craic?..15
Meet the neighbours..21
Whiskers...25
Home Sweet Home..27
Oliver's Mount...33
Cernunnos?..37
The Traf...49
Mine's a double..59
Keeping it Rial..67
Continental Circus, Hengelo..81
Sausage Schleiz...95
The Opposition..105
Suomi..111
Prague...129
No, really, what's the craic?..137
Me and my shadow..149
Czech-point Charlie..157
Frohburg..169
Rotten to the core..177
Fairy Bridge..197
Back to life, back to reality...211
Epilogue...221
The real John Willis..222
The Artwork...224
The Joey Dunlop Foundation...225
References..226

ACKNOWLEDGEMENTS

Scott Bowen
Trigger Bradshaw
Hari Burrows
Diana Campbell
Lisa Campbell
Winnie Campbell
Lynn Dean
Graham 'Genge' Elvidge
Lenny Hartley
Kev Hogg
Pavel Křižka
Steve Morris
Peter & Mariko Pojer
Tomáš Přibyl
Teigan Purvis
Anne Read
Steve, Debra & Stevie Rial
Sandra Roe
Pete Rumney
Rob, Vicky, Luna & Lola Simmons
Jay Smith
Paul & Andrea Stallard
Callum Wilson
Barry Wood

IMAGES

104 Books logo - Joel Neil Campbell
Author image - Lenny Hartley
Cover art - Peter Rumney
Daley Mathison Forget Me Not! cover image - Joel Neil Campbell
John Willis image - Teigan Purvis
John Willis logo - Rob AK Logo Designs

PREFACE

If you're reading this, my second book, hopefully you've purchased a copy or intend to. 'John Willis' is a change of tack from my previous offering. A Supernatural Humorous Espionage Thriller or SHET for short. If you've previously enjoyed 'Daley Mathison Forget Me Not!', never fear, there will be places and names familiar to you within this book.

Alternatively, if you're new to my fiction, join the club, so am I! I really hope you enjoy the story as much as I enjoyed writing it. It was a voyage of discovery from start to finish, so much so it would have been rude not to share it!

I would like to dedicate this book to David Knowles. A talented journalist at the Daily Telegraph, I only met him twice, on the same day. However, he inspired me through his work and his kind and caring personality. A link to David's obituary can be found in the reference section of this book.

Rest In Peace
David Knowles:
22nd September 1991 – 8th September 2024

I would also like to dedicate 'John Willis' to: Lisa, Mum and Winnie 'White Cloud'.

I started writing 'John Willis' whilst I waited for my first book, Daley Mathison Forget Me Not! to go through the publishing process. I was getting on my own nerves, obsessively checking my e-mail account day and night. Waiting for news, any updates or progress reports to drop through this virtual letterbox of mine.

The editorial, formatting and publishing process can take months and I'd been getting more and more impatient as each week passed. So, I'd been thinking about starting a new project, something to distract me. A chance conversation in my local pub was pivotal in kick-starting the process. That informal chat created a character which would quickly develop into a near fully fleshed out plot.

The details of that inspirational chat are featured towards the rear of this book.

It all came easily and the words began to flow. If I had to step away for a month, promoting and distributing the Daley Mathison book, I was able to pick up from where I'd left off with seeming ease. I'm new to all of this, so maybe I just got lucky.

If you were to ask me how to describe this book in one word, I'd reply: "It's a great steaming pile of S.H.E.T!" Cheating a bit using an acronym: Supernatural Humorous Espionage Thriller, but there you go.

It started out quite serious, intense, 'sciencey'. Is that even a real word? However, the characters, including aspects of my own, quickly took over, steering it slightly to the humorous side. That's okay, you can mix serious subjects with an undertone of mirth. Life requires both ingredients. Too serious, reach for the 'preparation H'. Not quite serious enough… well, you'll never realise your ambitions. Unless you're a budding comedian, I suppose.

'Write what you know' is an oft used quote and who am I to disagree? Whoever coined it, knew what they were on about, clearly. So, I have. Within the story are people, situations and locations that I frequent, based on real people and experiences that have happened to me. Maybe with a bit of artistic license to spice things up, or tone things down!

I'm a motorcycle road racing fanatic and as such there are places and situations from that environment which form the backdrop during several stages of the story. No need to worry, though, you don't need to follow or have any knowledge of that particular sport in order to follow the plot. However, for those aficionados amongst you, you'll recognise the Isle of Man TT, Oliver's Mount, Aberdare Park, Imatra and many other racing locations scattered across continental Europe.

If you've an interest in travel, admire the work of Judith Chalmers or whoever the current TV travel guru is, there are a plethora of locations to discover as you follow John Willis's exploits. Incidentally, I watch a lot of YouTube travel vlogs to get a sense of the atmosphere and surroundings of foreign shores that I'm yet to experience in the flesh.

In book form I've been inspired by the novels of John Le Carré, Peter F. Hamilton and Iain M. Banks. From the small screen I would lean towards The Hitchhiker's

Guide to the Galaxy (BBC TV series), Red Dwarf, Smiley's People (BBC TV series) and 3rd Rock From the Sun. At least as far as this book is concerned.

Hopefully with the inspiration provided by those listed above, I've helped to answer or achieved in part the following points:

I've long held the belief, the opinion that the two most important questions yet to be comprehensively answered are, in order of import:

1. What happens when we die?
2. Are we, the human race, alone in the universe?

Now, what if these two questions are related, and once linked provide the answer to both? Life, the universe and everything, and no, the answer isn't a number in the forties!

Whether I've failed or succeeded, well, it matters not. I enjoyed the process and hopefully, you, the reader, enjoy the book.

Cheers,

Joel.

ABOUT THE AUTHOR

I was born in 1970, Cyprus, RAF Akrotiri. My Dad was in the RAF at the time. We moved around a lot, Lincolnshire, Staffordshire, Hong Kong. We returned to Cyprus in 1981, Dad by then working for GCHQ.

I was a bit of a handful during the summer holidays. When I got too manic, Mum would make me write book or film reviews for the camp (Pergamos, formerly RAF Pergamos) newsletter. I'd sometimes win some voucher or money. I can't recall exactly which.

Dad covered sport for the Scarborough Evening news in his spare time, concentrating mainly on rugby union, but also the odd cricket or football match. Mum is an accomplished writer of short stories and poetry. Was it nature or nurture? Who knows. I seem to have some level of ability with the writing; time will tell how much.

I released my first book in the summer of 2024: a biography about Daley Mathison, the motorcycle racer who sadly lost his life following an incident racing at the Isle of Man TT in 2019. The Daley book was well received and I managed to sell all the copies, raising a not insubstantial amount for good causes.

I don't know where this journey will take me, but I'm enjoying the ride.

The author. Gold Cup 2020, Oliver's Mount, Scarborough
(Photo: Lenny Hartley)

JOHN WILLIS

ABERDARE ENCOUNTER

Picture a park, a very English Victorian park, although this particular one was located in the South of Wales. It was Friday morning, the calm before the storm. That would turn out to be an understatement of biblical proportions!

The storm I'd been excitedly anticipating was a weekend of motorcycle road racing, which would see this most tranquil of places transformed into a cacophony of sound. The quietude, the stillness in the air, replaced by that hard to describe, unless you've experienced it, sensation of being in the presence of speed. Your senses bombarded from all angles, fast bikes, cutting through the air, invoking strange sensations to body and mind. The sights and smells coupled with a contagious excitement spreading amongst the spectators washes over you, inviting you to submit, adding your energy to the groundswell of emotion, hard to resist. Unless, you're some type of emotionless drone, I imagine. That was to come though.

The park had been prepared for the event, protective hay bales placed, the starting grid refreshed with a lick of paint, timing equipment calibrated. Suffice to say, all the elements required to put on the show were in situ. I'd taken the opportunity to walk the track before it became a restricted area for the likes of me, a spectator. I'd been ambling along, at peace with myself, with life in general.

A burning sensation emanating from my left shoulder

blade snapped me out of my reverie. I'd experienced this before. I always took it as some type of warning. Of what, I didn't know. I rarely ignore my senses, preferring to investigate rather than brushing these things off. My attention was well and truly grabbed when I felt the hair of my crown standing to attention. I'd come to a halt, calmly reaching inside my pocket for my tobacco tin, all the while scanning my surroundings. Trying not to stand out, appearing as natural in my movements as I could, I observed a solitary figure about fifty yards further down the path. As I'd approached the stranger, the heat coming from my shoulder had spiked and then dissipated, curious indeed.

Seated on one of the many wrought iron benches overlooking a geese-filled boating lake was a man, let's call him Milton, for I didn't catch his name.

Milton was talking to himself, seemingly.

"Who are you talking to?" I asked.

Milton didn't raise his head, lock eyes with me, nothing like that. He just began to talk.

"Oh him, he tries to depress me, make me question my choices, do bad things to self and others. I ignore him, he gets frustrated. I'm a chess player, you know. He's wary of you, by the way. He thinks you are dangerous, protected in some way. He wants you to go away. Well, I'm censoring his true words. He's backed off, into the shadows."

A short pause then an invite was proffered. "Stay a while, so I can enjoy the silence for a time, sit! Sit!"

Quietude, well, apart from the geese, ducks and various birds chirping away.

"Is that him, it?" I asked.

"Where?" replied Milton, seemingly distracted.

"I saw a shadow, something dark pass behind that tree, over there."

"Oh! I see," replied Milton. "That's a cat, black. He's often milling about when I'm sitting here on the bench. We call him John Willis."

"Strange name for a cat?"

"It just came to mind. He isn't keen on him either. I like him. He may be black but he seems to bring light to the most miserable of days."

We sat in quiet contemplation for a while until with nary a word the man raised himself from the bench and, with a tip of his hat, he was gone. Not disappeared, you understand, in a puff of smoke. He strode off down the path that followed the boundary of the lake.

Only then did I notice his impressive silver topped walking cane, one of those African cold steel ones perhaps. Did Moriarty wield one? Anyway, the man cut an impressive figure swinging his stick as if to some brass band.

Funnily enough, he did pass by a handsome bandstand as he faded out of view. I expected him to click his heels, just my overactive mind. Who can blame me though after what some would describe as a weird experience. Not me… expect the unexpected.

He, Milton, never did ask my name. Maybe he knew it all along. If he'd enquired though, I'd have told him he could call me 'Whiskers', a nickname awarded to me by my pal, Jay. You'll figure out why he chose that particular moniker before too long.

RECRUITING THE 'SPECIAL ONE'

John Willis

Let me introduce myself, I'm John Willis. Well, that's the name I go by. Suffice to say I'm one of the good guys. If you were to put a label on me, you could describe me as an agent handler, case officer. I'd like to think I'm on a par with George Smiley, the clever, considered character from the John le Carrè novels.

Not for me all the drama, explosions, rolling across car bonnets... I'm the puppet master operating in the shadows. Don't get me wrong, I'm not sat behind some grand desk, half-a-dozen coloured telephones denoting my seniority! I like to be in the field, getting my hands dirty. I just prefer to go about my work in a subtle way, using the little grey cells, not kicking in doors and asking questions later. I'd also like to think I put the safety of my ward above the mission. There will always be another opportunity, time is on our side. Success or failure in our hands.

I'm here to recruit the man, one of the 'special ones'. Don't tell him I referred to him as a S1 though. I take many forms, sometimes a person, or a shadow figure, but currently I'm in the guise of a cat. Why? A bit of theatrical flair, for fun! What's life without a dash of whimsy?

I'll communicate with the man using my mind. Spooky, heh? A talking cat? This isn't a cartoon! I would only draw unwanted attention and freak the poor fellow out.

Carl Jung once elucidated about the 'shadow self'. He wasn't too far off the mark, our Carl. I'm definitely my own self though, not my shadow self. I think... let's get that straight!

I hope that's cleared things up. Still confused? Tough! Time to introduce myself to the man, again.

WE MEET AGAIN

John Willis, eh? A cat according to Milton. All I saw was a shadow, fleeting at that. Strange, very strange. Something didn't quite add up, felt a bit off. Nothing I could do about that, although I had a feeling, we, John Willis and I, would meet again. Ah well, this won't get the baby washed! Back to my digs, the 'Bute Arms'.

I lay awake at night, thinking about the full English… Welsh to come. I eventually drifted off into sleep only to wake in the witching hour, my bed enveloped by shadows surrounding, swooping. All was dark, but there were different shades of black, trust me because I certainly trust my own eyes. I've been there, seen this all before so I told them to go forth and multiply. As I was questioning that choice of words, I sank back into my slumber. You might think that I'm a tad blasé, indifferent to such a strange and spooky experience. Have no doubt, I take these things seriously, don't particularly enjoy them. It's just that I've experienced similar things throughout my life, thus far. I've tried not to acknowledge them, react in fright. That seems to give them, whoever they are, a hold on you. The more you open up, investigate and tune in, the more vulnerable you become. It's a dangerous game of cat and mouse. You don't, maybe never will have the full picture. Ignorance is bliss so they say. I'm not saying that I've been burying my head in the sand, sounds uncomfortable anyway. All that sand in your ear holes. I accept there are things beyond my ken. I've also, always been aware that at some point along this journey we call life, I may not have the option to shy away. These types of attack don't happen to just anyone, so I may have to fight back at some point. May, could, should. That's the problem when you're naturally inquisitive, but realise that you'll never completely understand the mysteries of life. Infuriating!

For now, I had the first day of the races to enjoy. I didn't experience any tingles or burning sensations, well, nothing paranormal related. I was too engrossed in my race day euphoria. Far too distracted by all the hullabaloo, the high-octane action, catching up with my fellow fanatics. Waffling on at ten to the dozen about this rider or that, discussing the merits of various shiny bits attached to particular bikes. Staccato conversations, suddenly halted as the bikes came into view and roared past, disturbing the air surrounding us. Picking up where we'd left off, now speaking twenty to the dozen, the better to finish our current topic before the pack came zooming past again.

I slept well on Saturday night, copious amounts of fresh air and a couple or three lagers ensuring a less dramatic eight hours of shut eye.

Sunday morning, the final race day. I leapt out of bed, ready to face the day, determined not to miss out on a single lap of action. Showered, dressed and fed – tick! I loosened the belt one notch and headed out for a constitutional. I found myself back at the bench.

No Milton this time. Not many people about just yet. I could hear the bikes in the paddock being warmed up, spotted a few keen spectators walking down the street, heading for the park entrance, orange clad marshals heading to their posts. Before too long, the place would be rammed, but for now, just me, the birds and my reverie. The world was brought back into focus, a feeling, a stillness in the air.

I noticed a flash of black out of the corner of my eye. Ah! The cat, John Willis, was back. He slunk towards me, looked up, caught my gaze and with one fluid motion positioned himself on the other end of the bench, distractedly cleaning one paw.

'Good morning.'

I heard it in my mind's eye, like a real voice spoken out loud. A pleasant voice. No particular accent. I could still hear the background noises of the park.

I slowly turned my head and stared at John. I laughed to myself and thought, 'What you talking about, Willis?'

The voice again. 'Ha! Amusing.'

I was not really shocked, more intrigued. I was pretty certain I wasn't cracking up. Strange things happen, so I decided to roll with it. Like I said earlier, peculiar happenings seem to be a theme in my life. My reaction is less fight or flight, more 'why is this happening, what does it mean?' In short, I was curious. Where was this going? Besides, this cat, John Willis seemed familiar to me. Pardon the pun, honestly, I don't do it on purpose.

He'd heard my Willis quip so I spoke to him in my mind. 'Good morning, John Willis. Is that correct?'

'Impressive, you catch on quick and yes, John Willis is my name.'

I'll take this at face value, I thought. I'm not going to insist he prove himself, get him to tap three times on the bench with his rear left leg. No! I wasn't going to sink to that level.

'How can I help you, John?'

'Ah! Capital, capital, you've hit the nail on the head. You can help me, help yourself. Not to over-egg it, but you can help a lot more people than just you and me.'

'Has any of this got to do with that man, Milton, the other day?'

John's reply was, as I would soon learn, typical of him. 'Loosely, yes, in a way, no in another way. In short, hardly at all.'

John Willis got down to brass tacks, a briefing of sorts. We conversed mentally, well, to be accurate he talked and I listened. If I did chime in, I was conscious not to move my lips in sync with the words I formed in my head. I didn't want to look like a ventriloquist or some bloke trying to balance two worms above his chin. Besides, if I did slip at some point, no one seemed to notice my facial gymnastics or the sight of a man and a black cat sat side by side for that matter.

The park was filling up now, people excitedly darting to and fro. The fervour of a hundred conversations added a charge to the air. And then the bikes began pouring onto the track, warm-up laps commencing. More movement, colour reflected on the boating lake as people dashed to the nearest or a favoured viewing point. John Willis seemed distracted. The mental conversation halted. Was it the cacophony of sound, the multitude of colours and reflections of movement dancing on the water's surface like a living, breathing Monet, just yards from where we were seated? Or something else? I felt that oh so familiar burning sensation on my shoulder blade again, my cap nearly springing off my head as my hair stood to attention once more. The atmosphere surrounding us may have been manic, but it felt like John and I were enveloped in a bubble of calm, the air deathly still. I instantly recognised this sensation. It wasn't entirely of John's doing. It was like being submerged in a hot bath. I imagine a sensory deprivation tank is similar. That comforting feeling that takes us back to the womb.

John's gaze swept over me, scanning from head to toe. I was about to ask him, out loud, what was going on. Instead, I watched his subtle movements as his head tilted, eyes now sweeping the opposite bank of the lake.

'We need to go. Immediately.' His mental tone left me in no doubt of the urgency of the situation.

As we rose from the bench and calmly headed to the crossing point opposite the bandstand, I sensed Milton's personality, his presence. Not physically. It was more of a mental impression. He was observing us, remotely. He may have been two hundred yards away or peering into a cauldron for all I knew. The point being I couldn't spy him amongst the crowd. I did, however, spot four blokes who looked distinctly out of place in both demeanour and garb. Slow, stiff legged movements, dark suits, no colourful team-wear adorned these, whatever, whoever they were. The fact that I didn't automatically associate these interlopers with Milton wasn't lost on me. No, these weren't his henchman, they were something other. Why would Milton have henchman in the first place? There was something off about him, that's for sure. Now is not the time, I admonished myself.

Fortuitously the warm-ups had concluded, the bikes returned to the paddock. The track was clear of any danger, safe for a temporary crossing point to be opened up to allow the paying public to make their way across to the other side of the track. The spectators were oblivious to the man and his feline pal making a bee-line to the ornate Victorian bandstand. Our quartet of suited friends were closing in on us, but they didn't have the fluidity of movement that we possessed. Three of our pursuers looked distinctly human as I glanced behind, all the while making sure I didn't stray too far from John. I worried that he'd be trampled at some point, but imperceptibly people seemed to part, like the waves, in his path.

I risked another peek, aware that we were closing in on the bandstand that John seemed to be heading towards. My focus was on the fourth member of the group. This one although similarly clad in dark attire had no discernible facial features. From the neck up, it was like he'd been pixelated out, like you sometimes see on YouTube in order to protect someone's identity. Blurry, hard to make out, even if I used the old squinting trick. This was no human, I understood on an instinctive level, this creature was different. I concluded that it was either very stupid or desperate to get to us, revealing itself in such a public setting.

As we arrived at our destination, John halted and turned to face our foes. They'd been thwarted, the crossing point closing as they jostled their way to the front. The first race of the day was just minutes away. The human type members of the gang seemed resigned to their fate, well aware that attempting to cross a live race track would not only draw unwanted attention here and now, but could also lead to criminal proceedings and exposure in the media.

The fourth member, old pixel bonce, he didn't seem to, or want to accept he'd been thwarted. He was obviously the leader, separated from the others by rank and race. However, it was these underlings who were attempting to mollify and move him away before he did something they'd all regret. I made a note of this petulant display. He may have been different, but he wasn't the sharpest tool in the box. I saw weakness, the polar opposite to the calm that John had displayed in reaction to a sticky situation.

'Come on,' John said in my mind.

I didn't even flinch this time! I had rapidly become accustomed to this new, to me, method of communication. Something else that felt vaguely familiar. We departed from the rear of the bandstand, by now full of spectators, funny sight really, when you think of it. And headed up the path which led to the paddock. About half way up, I followed suit as John stepped to the left. Out of nowhere, well, obviously somewhere, a portal opened up in front of us. A swirly, vertical, flat disk of energy.

Looks like a rainbow lollipop, I thought.

John stepped in. He obviously had no doubt I would follow, and duly, I did. I had to crouch a bit, mind you, not quite cat height, but I think I'll pop a note in the suggestion box before I use one, again, if there is a next time.

WHAT'S THE CRAIC?

We emerged close to the bench near the boating lake where we'd been so rudely interrupted just minutes earlier. Not much time had passed, but although the surroundings remained the same, the atmosphere bore no resemblance. No racing for a start, just an average quiet morning in the park.

Another point in time, I imagined, another reality, timeline? I was yet to understand how all that stuff works, still don't fully comprehend it. Perhaps it'll come with… time… groan!

John had confirmed my suspicions. "Yes. Same place, reality, just a different time."

For once, I took this at face value. However, I did have one question. "Does Milton possess, to pardon the pun, this same control over time and space, John?"

"Oh yes, performing the action is well within his abilities. Locating our present location is not. The law of averages should protect us, thwart him. If, by some miracle he was to find us, we'd just pull the same trick and be long gone before he even managed to curse our very existence."

John Willis, most probably trying to deflect or at the very least delay the inevitable barrage of additional questions, raised a paw and then swept it from left to right. The two movements I understood to mean: time to listen, learn and please be seated… or words to that effect.

We sat back on the bench and John resumed his briefing. However, this time, as the park seemed deserted, it was your standard, non-mind to mind chat.

Over the next hour or so, John described what was required of me, why I was being recruited and set about explaining how things really worked on this planet, this reality, this universe.

According to John, this was the current state of play:

There's a war going on, in the shadows, a millennia-long struggle between good and evil. It's developed into a cold war, a balancing act, maintaining the status quo so to speak.

On Earth, the Angels and fallen angels have been fighting over the souls of humans, the fate of humankind, ever since the rebel Angels were cast out of heaven and thrown down to Earth following their defeat to those led by the Archangel Michael.

Over time, the hot war has chilled and its current temperature is merely cold. Why is this? Well, the… let's call them the 'baddies'… realised that victory would only end in a type of defeat. The Angels faced a similar quandary… a final, decisive victory over evil would sentence humankind to a miserable fate, extinction.

The ultimate goal of Satan and his acolytes is to lead astray, deceive and ultimately exterminate as many of God's children as possible. But what happens post-victory? Where are the spoils? Satan and his pals will have lost their raison d'être. Yes, they'll have gained revenge on all the goody two shoes up in heaven, have a planet free of the human race, God's pet project. What now? No fun, boredom sets in. They'd most likely turn inwards and end up destroying each other.

Sounds like great news for the Angels, for humans? In the short term, yes. In the long term, a big old no. You see, humans need hardship, struggle in order to advance. War may trim the herd, cause pain and devastation, but it's one of the few activities that gets humans singing from the same page. It brings ingenuity, invention and ultimately progress that just wouldn't be possible in times of peace. Humanity had its own cold war in the second half of the 20th century but the one involving the Angels has been going on for centuries.

So, what is the end game? Humanity develops technologically, advances to the stage where they can leave home and ascend to the stars. Let Satan come with or stay on Earth and mess with the stragglers; he's the least of our worries.

You see, the thought of obnoxious, ill bred, antagonistic, destructive, verminous humans spreading out to all corners of the galaxy, the universe, maybe even dimensions, has not gone down well in the neighbourhood.

That was the general background, pre-empting the question forming in my head. John explained why I'd been recruited. I was dubious whether I could bring anything to the party, what with all these angels, demons and aliens about. I was just your average bloke, wasn't I? By the way, I'm pretty sure John has the ability to pick up on my thoughts when it suits him.

John explained that I had a particular gift that was vital to the cause. Apparently, I was able to sense the presence of xenos, long before John and his fellow Angels could. Time would tell, but he was confident that I would also develop the ability to both receive and transmit information to these particular aliens. In plain English, I'd be able to talk to them using my mind, and my early warning system had a far greater range than John's.

Xenos in the vicinity were indicated to me through the burning sensation on my shoulder blade and handily, John was also made aware of their presence as my Aura simultaneously lit up like a beacon. John's warning system, up to now, had been rather rudimentary. He could only sense them at a very short range, using something similar to the Transit method used by astronomers. This is where they observe a slight dip in the brightness of a star when a planet passes in front of it.

I'd hardly allowed myself to digest this information, when yet another set of questions barged their way to the forefront of my thought process. "But, why didn't they attack on Friday? Why now, when it's so much busier? Why, John Willis? Why?"

John Willis took or effected a deep breath before replying with the patience of a Saint, an Angel at the very least. "Why, why, why? Honestly, you've more whys than a Y-front factory! Too quiet on Friday, distractions today, everyone under the atmospheric spell that motorsport casts over this entire area. That is…WHY!"

Undeterred and hardly unexpected, I had one final

question, maybe two, for now. "So, John Willis, where does this Milton character fit in? Even I can tell he's no xeno. What was he doing there and who was the creature with the blurry swede?"

John frowned, obviously working out that 'swede' meant head. Milton, he'd explained, was a demon, obviously taking a watching brief, not directly involved. Perhaps he, or more likely his masters, were prepared to support the xenos in some type of proxy war. John indicated that the demons were well aware of me and most likely wanted to know why I was valued so highly by John.

"So, what was with all this talking to himself business, shadows, all that malarkey, John?"

"Ah yes, that. Quite quick witted for such a dim-wit. Not the most creative of imaginations our Milton. Well, none of them, demons, xenos possess an abundance of ingenuity. That's to our advantage. Helps us stay one or more steps ahead whilst they're blundering around like moths. That was me talking to him, mentally. Must have ruffled his feathers, rookie mistake on his behalf, vocalising, talking out loud. I knew more or less why he was here, just wanted him to know I was present. Ha! It certainly shook him off his stride. In a nutshell, I told him to sling his hook. Not the sharpest tool in the box, but slippery nonetheless. I certainly don't underestimate him, and neither should you. So much so, that I've got two of my best watchers keeping tabs on him as we speak. He hasn't left the area, but no matter, I'm curious to see what his next move might be."

I told John Willis that I thought the weird blurry bloke was some type of alien, his underling's humans. Yes, indeed John agreed, the blurry faced fellow was a xeno. His appearance had been surprising to him. He surmised that they were either extremely confident, or rather stupid, John leaning to the latter conclusion in this instance.

John rose from the bench, and I followed suit. Well, he leapt down, remember? Cat.

"Coast should be clear by now. Let's get back and watch the last few races, the presentations and such."

"Swirly time?" I replied.

An amused nod came my new friend's reply.

MEET THE NEIGHBOURS

John Willis

I'd given the man the basic good versus evil briefing, but had decided to save the alien angle for later, the whole geo-political machinations. For now, he knew a little of the xenos, their existence, his unique detection abilities and such. I'd expand on the whys and wherefores in the fullness of time, didn't want to bombard the lad. I had no doubt he'd digest and file away the information, take it in his stride. I was protecting my own sanity, avoiding an avalanche of questions. Besides, I wanted to watch the racing.

But this is what I knew regarding this new threat. For thousands of years, Earth has been visited by different races that come from near and far, relatively speaking. Some travel in physical form, some in the form of automatons, puppet-like emissaries. A few even travel here from and via different universes, from alternate realities. A veritable smorgasbord of creatures all with their own motives and idiosyncrasies.

Certain, let's call them aliens, have seen the war between good and evil as an opportunity. They've hijacked it for their own strategic reasons. They, the interlopers, have been meddling, impersonating, destabilising. They take on the form of demonic entities. Their goal? The complete and utter destruction and eradication of the human race. They foresaw the cooling of hostilities between good and evil and took it upon themselves to see the job through to its conclusion.

Don't misunderstand me. This involves just a handful of xenophobic races, who, as you would expect, can't stand the sight or smell of each other either. A handful it may be, but it only takes a few bad men, to paraphrase the old saying.

There are many other friendly or at least non-adversarial races who visit Earth, either in an official capacity – yes, you heard correctly – or merely as curious passers-by.

The physical form aliens, they're the less well-developed species, technologically, mentally. This may be a matter of time, a choice or they've just hit a developmental wall. Who knows? A million, squillion races, a billion reasons. Who cares?

They travel in some type of interplanetary vehicle, normally crewed by very basic organic puppet creatures. They don't need much in the way of rest or nutrients and have a brain well capable of delivering information and carrying out reasonably complicated tasks. They can think and make judgement calls based on the parameters set by their creators.

These species are in contact with various nations on Earth, and they too are interested in keeping the status quo. War is good for business. Wholesale destruction of the customer base and commodities is not.

They are interested in commerce, trading technologies, goods, minerals, hell anything, Koi Carp for all I know. They may seek certain technologies from us, stuff they haven't thought about before, electric toothbrushes or whatever.

Some higher-minded species who may have ascended from physical form, may use emissaries in order to collect cultural artifacts, poetry, music, stories.

There's a plethora of different weirdos in the universe, universes, and they all tend to end up here at some point in time and space.

We are dealing with advanced foes, depending on how you look at it. They are capable of manipulating time, space, dimensions, minds. If I had to explain how they manage that, I'd need a blooming big white board, a shed load of marker pens and after suffering the biggest case of tennis elbow known to man, you'd still be none the wiser.

WHISKERS

"You don't understand all this fabric, time, mind stuff, do you, John?"

"Well, let's put it this way, you're human right?"

"Yes."

"Do you understand entirely how your body works? How your organs, mind, nervous system function individually and collectively?"

"Well, no," I replied, sheepishly.

"Doesn't stop you being human, does it? Doesn't stop me doing my job," declared John, now grinning, arms spread, palms up.

"But, that's…"

John cut me off in mid-mumble. "We, nobody, can know everything just as long as we make best use of the knowledge we do have. Besides, if such a person exists, you know what they say…"

"Nobody likes a know it all!" I exclaimed, confidence returning.

"Correct."

"But aren't you celestial beings? Above all of this?"

"Well of course, but we get bored from time to time. We're above, below, behind such matters."

"So why does it matter?"

"It possibly doesn't, but we are the guardians, for want of a better word. We are duty bound to protect humanity and fight the forces of evil. In fact, anything that walks, talks and more importantly, thinks, has an innate understanding of the good/evil concept." John paused, probably anticipating yet another question, and with none forthcoming, he continued.

"Do you know what Jean-Paul Sartre is doing now? Right now, as we speak? Playing with his boules, overlooking the riviera with all his other existentialist cronies, pondering on the meaning of death. You see, you can talk and philosophise until the cows come home, but they've actually found meaning in their life… um… death. Whomever it may be, you, I, them, we, all need meaning to exist. Whether it's pointless matters not a jot. We choose a side, good or bad and without knowing the eventual result or effect, we do what we feel is right. So, let's crack on, eh? First things first, you'll need a codename."

"Why? I thought it was about time for another question."

John winked. I hoped it was anyway. I'd hate to think I'd given him a nervous tick already!

"I read it somewhere. It sounds cool anyway, don't you think?"

Okay then. "Whiskers," I suggested.

"Whiskers?" John tilted his head.

"Curiosity killed the…"

"Funny! Nonetheless, Whiskers it is!"

HOME SWEET HOME

I was going home, my home of Scarborough, early the next morning. No full Welsh this time. Got to look after the old waistline now I'm a fully-fledged supernatural agent I'd reasoned. To be honest, I felt like a fish out of water. Not sure what I'd got myself into, however inadvertently. What I did know was this: I was up for it. Deep down I felt like I owed John Willis, couldn't quite put my finger on what exactly, but I was resolutely determined not to let him down. Not going to happen!

As I exited the Bute Arms, John was perched atop the gleaming red bonnet of the van, basking contentedly, soaking up the early morning rays. I took this as a sign that he intended to accompany me on the not so short trek back up to the north east coast.

Beyond that, I was in the dark, no idea what his future intentions were. I was itching to know how I fitted into his future plans.

"So, I take it you're along for the ride? To sunny Scarborough? I know why I'm going. It's my home. Why you though, John Willis? Why not some city, at the heart of the action. That's where I imagined you'd base yourself."

"Curious indeed!" replied John. "Well, for one, I don't like the city, the majority of cities. Too clumsy. Dirty horrible things. A grimy bubble containing millions of farts, sweaty, stinky, too many sullen thoughts, no good. The pinnacle of planning? Pull the other one. Flawed really. The closer to the countryside, the better one feels, mentally, physically, spiritually. It's also much easier to pinpoint our foes. Don't get me wrong, we'll have to take the plunge at some point, head to the bright lights."

"London?" I enquired.

"Not necessarily, somewhere near to the madding crowd though."

During the journey, we drew quite a few amused looks and hand gestures, some obscene, from passing cars and lorries.

I presumed it was the little red van I was driving. John didn't help, sitting up on his hind quarters, innocently waving a regal paw: a 'Postman Pat' reference for those who are none the wiser. Got to laugh.

I broke the silence. "So why Aberdare?"

"Why Aberdare what?"

"Why did you choose Aberdare Park to make first contact?"

John scratched his chin with a velvet paw, indicating he was collecting his thoughts, either that or he just had an itchy chin. "Well, I knew you've been ready for some time, but it's only recently that the xeno problem has surfaced, in a meaningful way anyway. The current circumstances adding some urgency to the situation, we needed to get you on board, forthwith. I was aware that you were planning a trip to Aberdare to watch the motorbike races. Places, events like Aberdare, with its history tend to harness a lot of emotional energy over the years. In contrast to these short bursts of excitement and drama is the tranquil nature of the park in its day-to-day existence. These places, these race-tracks are a veritable melting pot of emotions, Whiskers. They tend to attract the types that like to feed off these energies, emotional parasites, vampiric in nature. Taking advantage of the shadows, lurking, waiting for the opportunity to prey on those they see as malleable. You see, I was also made aware that Milton, and his 'friend' the xeno, were planning on making an appearance. That convenient happenstance made my decision a great deal easier."

"Two questions…"

John interrupted. "Just two?"

"Funny! Number one: what are the sleeping arrangements. Stop smirking! Yes, I can tell when you're smirking, even with that poker face of yours, John. Number two: smirking again! You've explained why Scarborough, but for what?"

"You'll be doing your normal thing, Whiskers, at home with Lisa and Winnie. I'll be laying my hat at your Mum's, permission pending."

"How do you think my Mum is going to react to John Willis the telepathic super cat? And what exactly do I say to her, and Lisa? How do I broach the subject exactly?"

"Your mother should be fine."

I crumpled my face. "I never trust that word 'fine'. It's what kids say seconds prior to throwing up in the back of a car."

"Okay, she'll be alright? Better? She's a creative, she might think you've lost the plot, initially, but she knows you better than you think. Lisa with her medical history,

I've got that covered. I can monitor her and afterwards offer an implant that will resolve any further mishaps. I look after my team."

"Oh, so I'm one of many?"

"Slip of the tongue, old boy, slip of the tongue."

"How do you imagine Winnie, our West Highland terrier will react to you? She's friendly enough, but has been known to dismember the odd stuffed toy on occasion."

"Winnie will be fine… sorry, she'll be cool with it all. I'll send her calming thoughts, positive vibes, promise not to sniff inappropriately as long as she reciprocates. Besides, if in doubt I'll get the ham trim or cheese out! Dogs feel genuine love, affection, loyalty, fear, loneliness: base emotion type stuff. They don't ponder the meaning of life, stops them going rogue. Now cats, they think the big thoughts."

"A little bit biased, aren't you? Is that possessed cat starting to influence your thinking?"

"I'm not a possessed cat! No self-respecting feline would allow such an invasive and preposterous venture. This is just a form, Whiskers. To answer your second question. Your first assignment."

John Willis indicated the turn off to the Woodall motorway services. I parked up, switched off the engine, unclicked the seatbelt and reached to open my door. A paw tapped me on the shoulder.

A manilla envelope, tied with string was balanced on the dashboard. 'For your eyes only' stamped in red ink back and front; official looking and very Bondesque. I uncoiled the string and slipped a hand inside. Nothing. I peered inside: right first time.

I turned my head slowly to the left. Met John's stare. "Let me guess. You thought it would look cool?"

John returned an innocent frown.

"Pedal to the metal, young Whiskers, we've work to do. Time and tide wait for no man!"

OLIVER'S MOUNT

In spite of being handed an empty envelope, there existed two tasks on the itinerary.

Apparently, there was a portal in the vicinity of Dean Road cemetery, a bit on the nose, but that's where it was. I presumed I'd have to familiarise myself with it. I doubted it came with a manual. I didn't think I'd be pressing all the buttons and hoping for the best. I'd keep my hands firmly in my pockets.

The second more serious sounding objective was to take on and deal with some type of creature thing up at Oliver's Mount. I had only a fleeting knowledge of mythical creatures and the like, so John explained that some, not all myths, were in fact based in reality.

"There's a creature that calls Oliver's Mount his home. He's a fallen Angel in his natural form. For the purpose of his now hermit-like existence he's taken on the form of a cryptid."

"A cryptid?"

"Well, a cryptid is in essence a creature often found in myth or folklore, witnessed but never proved conclusively to exist. Think Big Foot or Nessie. It's quite a clever guise for a demonic or alien to embrace, a good role you might say. You see, if you want freedom to move around, within reason and you're leaning towards a solitary existence, it's perfect. It attracts less attention being a mythical, folklore creature than the alternative: alien in the woods, demon of the forest. It's yesteryear's news and the media, mainstream media, aren't interested, it's old hat. If anyone does spot him at night, for he sleeps during the day, no one takes the witness seriously. They've obviously lost the plot, had one too many or been nibbling the cheese at midnight. Incidentally, there is a cryptid called the Hat Man. You've no doubt met him at some point in your life, slumber, but I digress."

"I've met the Hat Man?" I think I'd have remembered that, I thought.

"He's a real weirdo that one, visits you at night, causes sleep paralysis, i.e. you're frozen with fear. Feeds on the terror of his chosen victim, tall, black, shadowy, not to mention the hat. A complete loser, Billy No Mates. Anyway, we need to deal with arguably a more pleasant if rather grumpy foe. This fellow lives up at Oliver's Mount."

"Another race circuit!" I exclaimed, not that I was complaining.

"Yes indeed, Whiskers, another race circuit. A lot of history and again places to lurk. This particular specimen has taken the form of a 'Deer Man'. The folklore would suggest the Deer Man is native to North America, but I suppose the global village encompasses everything these days. Regardless, it's an inspired choice. There's a herd of deer in residence at the Mount. This fellow can transform from scary-looking half man, half deer… the top half into a full-blown stag. He may use that form if he ever gets out of bed during the daylight hours. The real deer give him a wide berth though, bit wiffy, not keen on water or soap for that matter."

"But why is he in Scarborough of all places?"

"You'll have to ask HIM that, could be any number of reasons. Dropped out, got fed up being some type of demonic foot soldier, went a bit hippy dippy." John displayed double peace signs, not an easy task to perform, with cat paws. "Likes nature and made himself a nice hermitage by the sea. You've got fantastic views, near to town but far enough away, peaceful the majority of time and plenty of fish down at the mere."

"He sounds fairly harmless, John, why bother him at all? In fact, why do we need to use this portal thing either?"

"Well, this little confrontation will be a good warm up. It'll get the old blood pumping, get your head in the game. Anyway, he may be a bit on the docile side these days, but let's not forget, he's demonic, done his fair share of evil deeds over the millennia. He may have seen the light, but a couple of centuries of good behaviour hardly begins to make up for his crimes. So, sod him!"

"And the portal? Is that our preferred method of travel?"

"Not necessarily," he said, "but there may be times when you need to get away sharpish. When it's life or death, you don't really want to queue for thirty minutes at check-in or go for a browse round the duty free to pass the time. Bish-Bash-Bosh, portal, swirly effect and home. We'll take a wander later on. You can check it out. It might be wise to portal somewhere and back, get you accustomed to it. So, if push comes to shove, it'll be second nature."

I nodded in agreement. "So how do we defeat this Deer Man? Do we want to destroy this creature?"

"Wallop it in the gob with a branch, de-antler it, send it hurtling back whence it came, sounds like a plan. The truth of it is that I don't know yet, we'll play it by ear, Whiskers."

"Oh dear!" I replied.

"Oh dear indeed!"

CERNUNNOS?

We scoped out the Mount on a couple of occasions. This Deer Man, cryptid, whatever he was, never made an appearance.

We checked out the lay of the land during the daylight hours, while he was asleep.

I'd pinpointed the location of his lair to a dense area of tangled wood just adjacent to Oliver's Mount proper, between Mountside and Oliver's Mount Road.

I had sensed something there in the past when I'd walked up and around Oliver's Mount late at night. The rest of the area had a special atmosphere, apart from this one spot. It just felt bad and didn't half raise the hackles. If you can't work something out with logic, trust your senses, that's what they're there for.

I was pretty sure that John knew fine well where the lair was situated, but whether he did or not changed nothing, so I kept my beak shut.

I knew what it was, some sort of Deer Man. I was pretty sure exactly where he slept and where he played. However, I was none the wiser how to go about defeating the thing. What would defeat look like? I had no doubt I'd be victorious. Get me! I wasn't sure where this unfounded confidence had come from, but it was most welcome.

A week had passed and John hadn't yet named the day. I reckon his concept of time is entirely different to ours. Alternatively, and he might protest this, but I think despite saying the cat personae was just a form, he was beginning to warm to the role.

I went round to my Mum's on Thursday morning. It wasn't entirely unannounced although my ulterior motive was. I usually did some shopping for Mum at the indoor market on a Thursday. I'd have done this regardless and wanted to see her, but I was curious to see what the score was and also how John was settling in.

John and Mum were sitting alongside one another, looking out of the French windows onto the garden as I poked my head through the kitchen serving hatch.

I dumped the bags on the counter top, switched on the kettle, then it was the obligatory photo session, for Mum's journal. Posing with John, requests to stand near, far, one arm here, the other there.

"Stop pulling funny faces!" pleaded Mum.

Eventually she put her 'Big Phone' away, smartphone to you and me.

I think John was mollified by the prospect of more of Mum's homemade ginger biscuits. I just wanted a mug of tea and a woodbine, 'rollie' to you, as I strolled round the garden.

John Willis joined me, not for a Woodbine, the stroll.

"So how are you getting on at Mum's, John? When are we going to meet the Deer Man?"

"Lovely lady, lovely, bit noisy though, isn't she?"

"How do you mean?"

"Well, she crashes about a bit, doesn't she? I was trying to have a nap the other day, sounded like a Greek

Wedding was going off downstairs. Funnily enough she was emptying the dish washer."

"With a sledge hammer?" I smirked.

"Ah, you know of what I speak?"

"Very much so!"

John explained that he'd spent countless, pleasant hours snoozing the afternoons away. Basking on the window ledge in Mum's clubroom, soaking in the sun's rays, listening to Classic FM, hypnotised by the sound of Mum click, clacking away on her computer keyboard. John content just to stretch out, she writing her short stories or playing countless games of Freecell. Added to that, the aforementioned ginger biscuits, accompanied by a warm saucer of milk. The saucer was for John, you understand! Apparently favoured by, but not entirely good for our cat friends.

I doubt John is affected by any such affliction, real or imagined.

Blooming Nora! Living the life of Riley is Mr Willis!

We completed our garden stroll and headed back into the warmth. At an opportune moment, while Mum crashed about in the kitchen making the umpteenth cuppa of the day, I could hold it in no longer.

"Come on, John Willis, let's get our collective A's into G and go Deer hunting!"

"Slow down, smoke a cigar."

"Eh?" I was confused by John's response.

"Heard it somewhere, YouTube, some wise old cowboy or horse wrangler fellow."

"Wise words indeed. Got one?"

"A cigar? No, sorry."

"I guess it's just slow down then," I said, with mock disappointment.

"I understand you're itching to get stuck in. I've just enjoyed a bit of company and relaxation here. Don't stress though, we'll head back up to the Mount on Saturday morning. You'd best set your alarm though, it'll be around 3am."

"The witching hour?" I enquired.

"Something like that."

I left the pair of them to concentrate on their face stuffing competition and headed off home in my van.

We parked up opposite Mere Hairpin, near the sidecar paddock for those road racing aficionados amongst you. I'd suggested a spot down near the mere, so we could blend in with the handful of hardy folk who'd risen early to do a bit of angling.

John Willis was having none of it. "I'm not walking up that blooming steep hill, cat form or not."

I rolled down my window and lit up a nervous woodbine. John gave me a wee pep talk.

"The main thing to remember is not to be afraid. No, I'll rephrase that, manage your fear. You need to stay mentally strong, a mixture of logic and ingenuity, a dash of instinctive aggression. I can help with the rest, hocus-pokus, magic and such."

"Sounds simple when you put it like that…"

"Hardly."

"So why don't you fight this thing? In fact, why do you need me at all, John Willis?"

"Second naming me again. Must be serious. A good question though. Yes, you're right, I could quite easily sort this fellow out, well relatively easily. Let's not forget the bigger picture though, Whiskers. This is just one piece of the puzzle. You and I need to work together. It won't do either of us any good if I simply call you off the bench anytime I feel there is a possibility of xeno activity. Bear in mind, I don't possess the xeno locating gift that you have. I can't predict when they're going to turn up again and I most assuredly won't leave it to chance. Besides, the higher-ups want and actively strive for a human component in these matters. Before you ask, as you inherently do, I'm not entirely sure why. That sort of thing is above my pay grade, not beyond my ken, but not fully clear."

On that note, we set off in search of our prey. We weren't going to make a bee-line for his lair, he could be anywhere amongst the trees.

It was that strange time, when night transitions to morning. The moon was descending to its bed and the sun hadn't decided to rise yet, probably just hit the snooze button on his alarm. In short, it was dark, but not so that you couldn't accustom your eyes to it all. You'd better not hang about though, unless you fancied going A over T on some tree stump.

We climbed up the path on Quarry Hill, over the foot bridge, past the start/finish control tower and up past Jefferies Jumps, clambering over a couple of step-over gates, John slinking under. Then we cut up a little where the trees and foliage became more densely packed.

Shuffling, scraping, rustling... lots of 'ings' had me on full alert. I stood deathly still. John sat like he was waiting for the bus. Hairs on the back of my neck stood to attention, a feeling of being enveloped in an icy cold shroud, the swirly bit on the crown of my head tingling under my woolly hat.

A thud to my left, a rock or branch landing in a clump of wild grass. A distraction, I surmised, as I picked up a flash of shadow to my right. All of this was happening in the blink of an eye, but I was calm, felt in control. Time had slowed down. Composed, well, I was, then a flash of white. I saw stars as with a roar something tackled me head on. With a whoosh and thump to the chest, I was sent flying back in the air. Quite comical really, I thought, as I was being ejected from my previous position. I landed and came skidding to a halt on my backside. Not very dignified, but at least I wasn't sprawling.

A huge specimen of a creature towered over me, tall, muscular, hoofed human-like legs, torso, the head and antlers of a stag... I think, well, I don't know all the animals! Suffice to say, this had to be the Deer Man. Head to hoof a dark walnut hue, piercing red eyes strobing out from his craggy features. I didn't know what John was up to, nor cared. The creature arced over me, closing off my peripheral vision, enveloping me with his antlers. I already had the stick, twig, whatever grasped tightly in my right hand. Swoosh, I thrust the stick straight back along the strobing path towards his eye. Floop! Direct hit, laser guided accuracy. The creature stood erect, spun ninety degrees to the side, raised his antlered head to the stars and screeched like a scalded pig. I'd have expected a booming wail, but, touch wood, I've never been poked in the eye with a sharp stick. Talking of which, it was lying on the ground now, having been wrenched out and thrown by the creature. I picked it up. A smirk crossed my lips. There was an eyeball attached to the end. Looked like a marshmallow. I was still sniggering when 'pop', it disappeared out of existence. Deer Man had regained his composure, standing at his full height, back straight. His eye socket was enveloped by a wisp of white smoke and his injury was no more. Old red eyes was back in town. Just a mirage then, the pain was definitely real but the physical damage, temporary, an illusion. His eyes, both, were blazing now. Oh dear, seemed a bit, very annoyed now, whatever.

"Who dares to cause such acts of wanton sacrilege in this my holy domain?!" he roared. "Who befouls and trespasses where the Lord of the Wild Places calls his home?! For I am Cernunnos, God of…"

A familiar voice cut him off in mid rant, thank God! "No, you're not, you're Trevor, Trevor Herne. Well, that's what you go by, in certain circles," John proclaimed.

I glanced to the left, down a bit. John dipped his head and gave me a wink. I took this to mean well done and watch this.

With those words from John, the creature, Trevor, was stopped in its tracks. He slowly turned his head, angled it down dismissively towards John Willis.

"And who in hell are... oh, it's you!" as he visibly shrank in both stature and confidence.

"Yes, it is I! John Willis, Lord of the whatever! Master of the universe! Parum! Pum! Pum!" He pumped his tiny paw in the air.

Trevor, resigned and for all intents and purposes a beaten man, deer, Deer-Man? slumped to the ground, legs crossed, lotus style.

John began gently interrogating our Trev. You catch more flies with honey than vinegar, sometimes. Over the following twenty minutes or so, John enquired as to what Trevor was doing here, in Scarborough, and why Oliver's Mount?

Trevor explained that he'd descended into a hermit-like existence, ashamed of his past, wanting to atone in some small way. He'd been trying his best to keep demonic activity to a minimum, discouraging any xeno infestations, keeping an eye out for any comings and goings at the portal.

At the mention of 'keeping an eye out' I'd barely managed to contain a snigger as I had a flashback of his marshmallow-like eyeball attached to my stick. Not seeming to notice my facial, muppet-esque contortions, Trevor explained that he even discouraged, in his unique way, any destruction, vandalism or littering at the Mount, the Mere and the area in general.

He said that he spent the rest of his time watching over the Flora and Fauna that call the Mount their home, although, by and large the animals tended to give him a wide berth. Of course, they were curious initially. That idle, corner of the eye curiosity, but now treated him with indifference, part of the furniture.

Satisfied with this explanation, John agreed to leave Trevor in peace, dependent on certain assurances. He was to ensure no harm came to both my Mum and Lisa, not forgetting Winnie of course, while we were away galivanting, ensuring the safety of everyone's loved ones… and pets!

John also quizzed Trevor on any recent activity down at the portal and encouraged him to be even more vigilant in that regard and to keep us appraised the instant anyone poked their snout in or out of that location.

So that was Trevor dealt with, recruited. He seemed much relieved as he trotted off, once more enveloped by what was left of the night.

John Willis licked a paw, drew it over his scalp, turned to me and spoke. "Come on then, no point hanging about, besides I'm starving!"

"Ginger biscuits?"

"Bacon sarnie! HP sauce! Saucer of tea."

"No arguments there, I'll take a mug though, feel daft on all fours," I joked, no saucer for me, thank you very much.

We headed off in silence for all of two minutes, before curiosity got the better of me, as per.

"Why Trevor Herne?"

"Oh that. A lot of these creatures adopt non-descript, bland monikers. It's in order to distance themselves from previous heavenly misdemeanours."

"Like John Willis perhaps?"

"Careful now, cheeky chops!"

"And Herne?"

"Well, evidently our Trevor hasn't lost all of his mischievousness. Better brush up on your Shakespeare."

I must either have looked at John quizzically or he picked up on it mentally.

"Just google it!" John Willis grinned like a Cheshire cat. He knew fine well that I always said that when bombarded with questions, a bugbear of mine.

In harmony, mentally, in our head voices, 'If you're that curious, look it up for yourself!'

Grins all round. "Point taken," I said, out loud.

When we got settled back in the red van, the conversation took on a more serious tone… well, less jovial.

John grabbed my attention with a raised paw.

"You did well out there…"

"We both did…" I replied, modestly.

"Yes, yes. The point I was trying to make, before being so rudely interrupted!" exclaimed John, the accompanying grin indicating amusement rather than irritation. "The point I was attempting to make, is that you're developing exponentially, you perceived that the rock thrown by Trevor was a feint. You did this out of time, in a bubble of calm, so to speak. You shouldn't have been able to inflict an injury on such a creature. By the way, marshmallow! Hilarious!"

John continued with his praise heaping. "I think, forgive me, I know that you managed to affect him somehow, through raw mental strength. Would you have been able to defeat him alone? No, not at this stage. Could you have escaped with all dangly appendages intact? Most likely. Right! No rest for the wicked. Home, James! I require bacon, immediately, now!"

THE TRAF

We headed to Mum's after departing Oliver's Mount, stopping briefly at Nige's shop to stock up on bacon and bread buns. I did the honours, appetites satiated, mine anyway, not sure if John suffers from hunger pangs, doubt it. It was time for a wee nap, I needed a kip after our adventures on the Mount. John Willis again although probably not requiring any form of rest, was not opposed to the idea.

I suppose even beings such as John need to rest their brain, mind, whatever his physiological equivalent is. Thoughts and actions still need to be analysed, indexed and the like.

I'd laid my hat in the box room, John in the 'clubroom' bedroom. After a couple of hours, we had shaken off our slumber, wiped the sleep from our eyes and had set off into town. Not before the now traditional photo shoot.

"Why all the photos?" asked John.

I just shrugged my shoulders in reply.

Off to Lisa's house we went. As we got out of the van, we spied Winnie looking out of the bedroom window, carrying out her neighbourhood watch duties, which inexplicably required her to lick said window from time to time. Seeing the pair of us, I noticed her withdraw from sight, probably thudding down the stairs to greet me and loudly request some ham trim or piece of cheese.

Lisa took to John Willis remarkably well and rather

than retreating into a mute, shocked state could have happily chewed his ear off for hours. Winnie took a little more persuasion, at first hiding under the settee, tail tucked, ears flat.

John must have sent her soothing mental thoughts and images of pork and dairy products, for she soon perked up. John, having forewarned us and left the room, returned in the form of a slightly shadowy, tall slender man.

Once he'd led Winnie to the fridge and saved her from starvation, always hungry that one, he had a friend for life.

Winnie trotted off back into the lounge to catch up on her soaps with Lisa, and John and I chatted in the kitchen while I had a woodbine at the back door.

John Willis seemed distracted by the chaotic scene adorning our dish rack.

"What sort of chaos theory explains that debacle?"

"Don't get me started on that," I replied, resignation etched on my face.

"For a minute I thought you had a poltergeist in residence!" he said, amusement enveloping his features, the little that were on display.

"You've seen the fridge?" I enquired.

"Oh yes. Anyone for a game of Tetris?"

"Not advisable," I cautioned.

"At least you've managed to get the stairs cleared, no plethora of items making their way glacially to the top landing."

"Have you been here before?"

"No, Whiskers. Not my first rodeo though."

I finished my woodbine and turned to John. He must have, probably did, read my mind.

"Pub?"

"Oh yes, oh yes indeed!" I agreed.

Lisa was engrossed in some drama. I call them her gravel-voice programmes, lots of serious people being all overly-dramatic. 'You better watch your mouth, Wayne. Don't ever cross me or my family!' That sort of thing. And with Winnie's hunger temporarily vanquished, we shouted our goodbyes and put our best feet forward, not feet and paws on this occasion.

En route, which is only a five-minute stroll, three, if thirsty, John explained how he managed to enjoy his food and drink given he had no digestive system or tastebuds to speak of. He absorbed any solids or fluids into the body of his form and over the years had probed, recovered, experienced the sensations and tastes and textures of things.

He had a huge mental library of all sorts of delicacies, but admitted that he liked good home-cooked food and normal drinks, not cocktails and things that took longer to make than to drink.

"I know you've morphed into a man type form," although I noticed his gait retained a languid feline quality, "but will it pass scrutiny in the Traf?"

"People see what they want or expect to see, or are too wrapped up in their own thoughts and deeds to notice," explained John.

We walked through the lounge side door at the

Trafalgar Pub, a couple of smokers parting to allow us over the threshold. I headed to the bar as John, shrouded in a light grey shadow, slunk over to the corner next to the gambling machine, admiring the large Battle of Trafalgar mural on the way.

Now at the bar in eye catching mode, I realised I hadn't asked John what he wanted. A word/image formed in my head, Guinness, what else? Dark and smooth.

"Your mate old enough?" asked the barmaid, in jest.

"Oh, he's plenty old enough, on his ninth life that one."

The barmaid winked and retreated to the public bar to serve the next thirsty customer.

John had overheard my nine lives quip.

"Funny."

"On that subject, of age, exactly how old are you, John?"

"Well, I'm really not entirely sure. Everyone stops counting after twenty-one, don't they? Let's say I'm older than twenty-one, younger than that rock formation over there."

"There isn't a rock formation anywhere near here!" I exclaimed.

"Not that you can see... old boy."

Hmm, I wondered if John could visualise this place in different eras, in real time? Flick through the decades like searching for a document contained within a living filing cabinet. No, that was giving me a headache, I'd ask him some other time. Priorities, Whiskers, enjoy your blooming pint.

Time to relax, savour our drinks, sit back and people watch.

The landlord and landlady were holding court in the lounge bar. Verbal thrust and parry, egged on by the regulars gathered at the bar. A light-hearted Punch and Judy show. Well, we were beside the seaside; I do like to be beside the sea!

The pub was a hub of activity: the thump, thump of the darts nestling in the board, a chorus of 'sing it baby' each time someone scored a 180, which happened surprisingly regularly; excited whooping in the public bar; a game of pool in full flow; sage advice and x-rated criticism dished out in equal measure. Added to all these activities, the omnipresent ebb and flow of that indiscernible murmuring, humming, of a dozen conversations and raucous laughter that permeates the British 'local'.

All this kerfuffle added layers of distraction to John's shadowy visage. I'm sure he could have taken on a more natural human form if he'd wanted to, I think he just enjoyed the theatre of it all. I, not for the first time, albeit with more clarity, started to notice the odd shadowy outlines of figures, flitting to and fro as if trying to get served, catch the barperson's eye, earwigging a conversation between drinking buddies.

John explained that these were human spirits, pub regulars, some from the recent, some from the distant, past. Some that I'd recognise, others hazily familiar, the rest, not so, drinking an imaginary pint, real enough to them though, nibbling on pork scratchings. Even in death, cautious not to chip a tooth. Have you heard how hard it is to get a dentist these days? No such problems for them. Takes time to shake off physical worries though. Desperate to join in with the banter, reluctantly drifting to an unoccupied back rest, stool, nook or cranny… handicapped by their state of being, happy nonetheless to be on the periphery, involved in any way, however small or inconsequential the part. Some popping in and out of this reality for a quick pint, the latest gossip… others, who've never moved on, ignored the call for last orders, content to hang around. A spiritual lock-in. Dinner must be in the dog by now!

After several more pints, me insisting on paying, John not arguing the point, I suggested a leg stretch.

"Corp club for a game of snooker?"

"I'll pass. Besides, it's bingo tonight."

How, I questioned myself, was John a regular down at the club I called my own?

Sensing my surprise John Willis explained. "This isn't my first visit to Scarborough, Whiskers. I've frequented most of your haunts over the years. We have similar tastes you and I. Before you ask why, I think you already have some semblance of an idea. Besides, we're out for a pint. I assure you that I'll fill in the gaps. Let's not talk shop, relax and enjoy your beverage." As an afterthought John declared, "Fascinating game though."

"Bingo?" I couldn't imagine John studiously studying his card, 'dabber' poised. Never said he disliked the game though.

"Snooker!" came his indignant reply.

Back out on the street, fresh air filling our lungs, making my stomach feel empty, 'squirgling' noises pleading for attention.

"Fancy something from the chippy? Some fish?" I asked.

"Not on this occasion, Whiskers. I've a hankering for a battered sausage tonight."

"A Linford and chips, gotcha."

"Why do you call it that… no, it's okay, I understand now, oh my! On the subject of fish though, do you know that the alien puppets, the automatons, reek of it?"

"They smell fishy? Why?"

We'd arrived at 'Carol's Plaice' which is just round the corner from the Traf and just down from Lisa's. We halted our alien, fishy conversation whilst I ordered our tasty treat and John sat outside on the bench. All sorted, the chips were tucked under my arm, keeping me warm like an oily, delicious hot water bottle, wrapped up in paper, hot to the touch.

John took up the thread. "Well, fish smell… fishy due to a molecule called Trimethymaline N-oxide. TMAO for short. This clever little mechanism helps to stabilise the proteins fish use to build and maintain their cells. The deeper the fish live in the ocean, the higher the pressure and the more TMAO they produce. Without all this stuff they wouldn't be able to cope in high pressure environments, the cells would distort and the animal would die."

"Glad I had the pie!"

"Indeed."

"So, the alien connection?"

"Well, those alien puppets, although pretty basic lifeforms in terms of internals, still have to endure high G situations which would take a heavy toll without these clever molecules. Their ships obviously have various systems, fields, inertial dampening devices. If these fail, they really don't want to get mushed up, lose control and go careering into the side of a mountain, or some desert 'AREA'..." John wiggled his eyebrows, Marx Brother's style.

Forgive me, I was still getting used to all of this. He didn't physically do the eyebrow thing: it appeared in my mind's eye.

John continued. "Actually, the little grey chaps aren't obsessed with secrecy and disclosure. It's your lot. The greys are capitalists at heart and want to open up their markets. They don't see the sense in dealing exclusively with these bureaucratic institutions, locked into rigid contracts."

This was all fascinating to me. I should take John to the pub more often. "Why don't they just tell the powers that be to get stuffed, land during the opening ceremony of the Super Bowl? Scratch that. People would just think it was some advertising skit by Budweiser. You get what I mean though?"

"Well, for one thing, there are only a handful of grey-type races represented here on Earth and although they want more freedom, they're in a quandary. They'd like to open things up, but they fear they'd lose their current slice of the cake. If word got out, many more, equally greedy, species might start arriving in their hordes. You could say it's a case of having your cake and eating it too. Secondly, they've sold you, unwisely in my opinion, their most valuable technologies. They now class some nations here as peer adversaries, should, God forbid, hostilities break out." A pause, not for breath, I don't think John requires that. "Thirdly, they aren't big gamblers, rather on the conservative side. Comes with age. Risk averse. They need what we've got, and what they require would almost certainly be wiped out and lost if it came to blows. And before you ask what they need, I'll fill in the gaps another time, our chippy tea is getting cold."

MINE'S A DOUBLE

Well, the evening in the Traf bore fruit. For one thing, pint, for another, chips. What's not to like?

I found out some more about what's going on, discovered new things about John Willis, all extremely useful, John's apparent penchant for Bingo aside.

I'd also developed my senses a little bit, picking up on the various ghostly visitors to the bar, receiving John's Guinness order. No! not 'McPint', one for the bike fans there. Small steps, granted, and I'm not entirely sure how much John was involved in these revelations, my preternatural education.

In plain English, can I read John's thoughts now? Or is he enabling it? I doubt everyone can tune into John Willis FM or Radio Whiskers for that matter. Some part of it must be down to me, another series of questions to bombard John with, nice! What next then? I thought to myself. No point asking John. He's far too content whiling away the days at Chez Mum.

•

John Willis here. He's a cheeky one my protégé, isn't he? Not that I feel the need to defend my apparent lack of action, but I'll explain myself anyway, just for the record, you understand? I'd given young Whiskers a few tasks. I mention this because you might think I'd been resting on my laurels, not getting the show on the road. Well, whoever said, 'There's no time like the present' obviously needed to get out more, or better still, stay in more; read, study, ponder and figure out exactly how things work around here, 'Life, the universe, and everything'. Besides I was relaxed, enjoying these rare moments of quietude, periods of relaxation. Don't worry though, it would soon be time to make a break, make a move.

•

John had provided me with an answer to my question, cough, cough, alright questions! I was going to school: a crash course. He wanted me to start developing my skills, senses, communicating mentally with John, locally and from a distance. I spent more time around others, feeding off the emotions of strangers. A bit ghoulish really: like a parasite, leech, a mental vampire.

I could feel myself, I think, becoming more attuned, dialled in to what was going on around me. I don't know if these, let's say attributes, are dormant in all, ready to be triggered. All I know is that I felt different, seeing with more clarity, like my mental periphery had expanded its boundaries. Yes, I know it all sounds a bit far out. Don't worry! I haven't lost the plot, yet.

I used every opportunity, planned or otherwise, to push on, improve. I admit that I was playing things by ear, but I was making a concerted effort not to second guess my methods, just trying to do what felt natural to me. If you can walk tall, project confidence, then some of those cocksure particles must reflect back on you. I felt like I was making progress, on the right path. That's all you can ask for really.

So, it was off to The Blacksmith's Arms in Cloughton, a pub of the old school, centre of the community within the Duchy of Lancaster. Times they're a changing, but the Blacksmith's retains all that's good from the past. Not to fear though, they aren't stuck in the dark ages. Mind you, the internet was temporarily absent without leave. Quite refreshing.

By the way, I wouldn't be surprised if the landlord has some sort of 'spirit' ability, pardon the pun. He asked me where, when he remembered me from, in this pub, I presumed.

I told him, from the late 80s on reflection, 1987 to be precise. I failed to mention I was seventeen back then, for they were different times. I couldn't have crossed any line though, failed to follow pub etiquette. When you were of that age, you watched your Ps & Qs, kept your trap shut, no swearing, scrapping or spewing. Well, if you knew which side your bread was buttered.

A pint, a meal, delicious! No square plates, miniature chip fryers, pots of this, drizzles of that. I was happy, in a reverie, a short-lived one.

I sensed a presence, an old fellow, retirement age. Well turned out, voice a whisky-smooth Scottish drawl: Edinburgh at a guess. I saw through the deception, playing the 'bar bore', holding court, reciting not unfamiliar tales, young 'uns' listening politely as if for the first time. It's a good cover, I thought to myself. Paradoxically centre of attention but easily dismissed, forgotten, not a threat. I said 'bore'... that's a little harsh, we all catch ourselves re-telling, recounting a favourite memory, it's no crime. The man, for this was a bona fide man, wasn't here to entertain, he was here to make contact, with me. He must have some sort of gift, I thought, maybe a sidekick? I glanced around, nothing. I sensed him, before seeing, laying eyes on him as I returned from an après meal woodbine.

As his reluctant entourage slipped away, home, polite excuses or on to the next watering hole, I took up a berth at the bar. Standing gives off an air of confidence as opposed to slouching on a stool. Arms wide, palms down, making sure to scan for spillages. The double agent nursed his double Glenfiddich.

I ran a discreet eye over him, studying his countenance in the bar mirror. He had a reflection at least, that's a plus. No cloak or dagger on display.

Pah! Don't mirrors deceive as a principle anyway? Flipping left to right? No, no, it's front to back? You get the gist anyway.

I may not have a sweet tooth, but the proof is in the pudding, or so they say.

We talked, corner of the mouth talking, looking straight ahead, like two blokes at the urinals. A strange experience chatting to someone via a mirror when you could see both parties, you and him. It was like eavesdropping on yourself. Very odd!

My instincts were right, the Scotsman, let's call him Donald, was an agent of sorts, but this one definitely wore his 'troosers'!

Obviously, he didn't pronounce to one and all, 'Hello I'm Donald, I'll be your double agent today.'

He knew who I was, was aware of my mentor, John Willis. He was pretty much on the same page as John in regards to the way things really worked on the planet. He was aware of the parties involved, the motivations and machinations at play.

That was all very well, but what did I know about him? I'd had no brief, no file to peruse. So, in keeping with that theme, the no-messing-about nature of our conversation thus far, I unloaded my barrage of questions. You know by now that I'm the inquisitive type, and no, that's not a clever word for nosy.

"Who are you? Who are you working for? What are your motivations?" I asked.

Could have been a diplomat, don't you think? Not a very good one, granted.

Donald was a travelling salesman of sorts, a fixer. In a world without scheming aliens and the like, you'd describe his remit as industrial espionage, sometimes above-board, other times more on the shady side: arranging contracts, licenses to manufacture, transferring technologies, handling end-user license agreements, working on behalf of government departments and big business. Have briefcase, will travel. Donald owed loyalty to no one, only to those currently paying for his dapper attire and comfortable lifestyle.

Was he a double agent, or simply a wide boy? Lining his own pockets? Out for what he could get!

Did it matter, to me?

Not really. It all boiled down to one thing... could he help us?

He was provocative in an 'agency' sort of way. Not here accidentally. Double maybe, but with information to be bought and sold.

He worked for both the government and the greys, passing the latest information about the xenos between the two parties. The government and the greys were obviously in regular contact, but they didn't disclose everything to one another. They did like their secrets. Besides, the two Gs, while not exactly competitors, were involved in the business of trade. It was big business and when you sat down at that dealing table, you didn't lay all your cards face up when it came down to it. You wanted to walk away from there, to your Bentley or flying saucer with a spring in your step.

Donald's masters were well aware of his subterfuge. He'd be provided with kosher information, disinformation and something in-between. It was all a bit silly and confusing and the truth got lost at times, but he followed his orders and kept his various paymasters happy. However, that was just the big business waltz, when it came to the xenos, that affected both parties' interests. It was bad for business.

He'd been given carte blanche to assist us on our journey, in our quest, pardon the Lord of the Rings tone, hah! Ring tone! Anyway, back to the serious stuff, sorry.

Did I trust him? His motives? Less than I could physically throw him, a living breathing caber, I chuckled to myself.

Doubles were inherently untrustworthy. The only thing I could guarantee was that he'd be out for himself. I wouldn't lend him a tenner until payday. That's for certain.

Who knows? He could be a treble agent, playing the government, the greys and the xenos off against each other. Very dangerous, extremely unwise, but greed did tend to promote stupidity.

I was sure John would be able to see through the lies, half-truths and conclude whether Donald was to be trusted. I'll rephrase that, obviously he couldn't be fully trusted. John would decide whether we used him to our advantage.

I got the impression that Donald knew John by reputation, so I reckoned he fully expected his card to be marked if he stepped out of line. Nevertheless, anything he did from here on in would provide us with useful intelligence, whether he was assisting or betraying our cause. If he did happen to be in contact with xeno agents, all well and good, he'd lead us straight to them, save us a lot of messing about.

Long story short, Donald put us on a track, but more about that later, destination Eastern Europe.

Just a bit of admin now, tidy some loose ends up.

In another pub, you may well ask. Well, I do other things, you know! Besides, this was a family meal, a birthday celebration. No, I'm not being defensive, much. You get those people in the pub who sidle up to you. 'You're always in here, every time I come in here, I see you!' Well, duh! Fred, maybe I also see you, every time blah blah etc… perhaps we're just both on the razz more than we should. Apologies, soap box returned to the cupboard under the stairs. Mine's a pint!

I had to find John Willis. Not difficult. Brief him on the latest, make sure my passport wasn't out of date.

It was time for a jolly!

KEEPING IT RIAL

I'd been tasked by John to develop a cover story, something to explain our upcoming gallivant across the European continent. I was unsure why we needed one in the first place and secondly what story would hold up to whatever scrutiny John envisaged.

I wasn't ignorant of what one was. I'd read enough spy novels, hadn't I? Talking of ideas, the formation of an idea, do we really, truly experience divine inspiration? Or does the end product, the idea, consist of fragments, pieces of a jigsaw, that all come together when the need arises? Anyway, I digress. Get used to it.

To cut a long story short, temporarily… I was sitting on a train at Scarborough station, waiting to depart, heading for Beverley. My mate, 'Genge', would be boarding at Seamer station, on the outskirts of Scarborough.

Something about Sunday-running for buses… it was a bank holiday weekend, preventing him from getting into town on time. My shout, ticket-wise then. Luckily, they were doing a 'Duo' offer, 25% off as long as you travelled there and back together. Siamese twins, joined at the hip, don't wander off, fall out. No chance of that!

Don't misunderstand me, Genge wasn't ducking his duty, lumping me with the ticket fare. He was the most generous bloke I knew, too generous in my opinion. Ha! He'd be fuming when I told him the train was on me!

It turned out the joke was on me though! No victory this time. It was raining when we arrived at Beverley, the Minster looming over the rows of terrace houses. We dipped into the closest pub, and before I'd put lager to lips, I had Genge's rail contribution nestled in my upturned palm, a tenner and fiver, mocking me. You have to laugh.

A couple of pints and the sun was starting to beat back the slate grey clouds, rain already in full retreat. We headed into the centre. He, Genge, was starving, as per.

The Minster came into view again, spires cutting through and dispatching the angry clouds. A fragment of an idea formed.

"Let's go and have a look at the Minster," I suggested.
"Seriously?"
"Yep, my friend was in charge of restoration and stuff for years. Retired recently. I read his book about it, want to see it for myself."
"Let's do it!" exclaimed Genge.
What a place!
We were both blown away, the craftsmanship, the dedication that it took to create and maintain such a building. Awesome!

We headed off, destination Beverley market square, drink, food the order of the day. During the next couple of hours, another idea formed, a great idea! A pleasant afternoon was had by one and all. A few pints, sausage, egg and chips, over-loud pub TVs screening the Hull v Hull KR rugby league match.

To me, the TV, the noise, was all background, at the edges of my perception. My focus was dialled in, concentrated on this idea that was taking shape.

How do I explain this feeling, hmmm? Imagine looking at a large painting, of a scene, in this case a pub, but the image is your reality, you're sitting just out of frame though, but there. Time, noise, people around you are all slightly hazy, on the periphery. You're so focused on an idea, a thought, that it's like your brain is using so much processing power that it has to turn down the resolution on everything else. From high definition to standard. Anyway, suffice to say I was in a world of my own.

By Jove! I had it, the cover story. Time, noise, reality came flooding back in, whump! I was back in the room. How long was I in this trance-like state? No one seemed to have noticed. I was obviously great company, always looking like a stunned mullet, not standing out in a crowd!

Beverley Minster, Steve Rial, Road Racing News, the International Road Racing Championship, the IRRC for short.

These were the puzzle pieces, now I just had to put them together, set things in motion. I decided to sleep on my idea. If it still felt right in the morning, then it had to be the way to go.

I popped round to Mum's, found John in his favoured spot in the clubroom and presented the cover story. We would approach the Rials.

They were all, Steve, wife Debra and son Stevie, involved with Stevie's Road Racing News business. They covered motorcycle road racing, the youngest was the writer, the journalist. Steve concentrated on the photographic side and Debra was involved in the merchandise.

I would propose that myself and John would cover the IRRC for them, me the words, John the images. I'd written various articles in the past, was fairly proficient and John, he could turn his paw to anything.

The IRRC took place between May and September, featuring six race meetings, in five different countries. More importantly, the races were hosted exclusively on the European continent. This was perfect, we'd be travelling and working under the RRN banner, filing race reports, everything above board. On average there was a four week window between rounds. We could either return home, re-group or wend our way to the next location. Whose business was it if we stopped en route to battle with some eight-beaked alien lizard warrior or interrogated a demonic purple hamster. We had our cover story!

We didn't have to drag my family deeper into our crusade: we were off on an adventure, a road racing one.

Up to this point John was most definitely on board. How could I tell? He hadn't interrupted me, yet. I informed him that as far as the Rials were concerned, this was work, we were reporting on the IRRC. That's all they needed to know.

John's tail started swaying cobra like, left to right. That's agitation, annoyance in a cat. It promptly stopped and he lay down to rest. He'd obviously picked up on my internal smirking.

I explained that in my opinion the Rials were that

rare breed, just pure good, kind. You sometimes meet a person and you can tell instinctively that they have no side to them, no ulterior motives, just pure white light. I'm not saying these people you meet, rarely, are holier than thou, that's not the point, this is natural goodness. Don't worry, you can still have a pint, a joke, a laugh. Well, I found this trio were all of that ilk and I didn't want to expose them to anything dark, and that was the bottom line!

"We'll meet them at the next race meeting at Oliver's Mount, put forward our proposal and you'll see exactly what I mean. Trust me, John."

John dipped his head in approval, his eyes locked on mine.

I winked, poked out a tongue.

John Willis stretched, curled round, like a furry Danish pastry, and went back to his deeply important contemplations.

I did receive a message in my mind. 'Well done, Whiskers… purrfect…' I could visualise a riposte equal to that of my earlier cheeky tongue poke.

I'd already been in contact with Steve, testing the waters, but I preferred to elucidate on my idea in person. The next race meeting was only a fortnight away. I say only, it felt like an age.

In the meantime, I did a little homework, checked out the various locations we'd be visiting within the framework of our racing assignments. I'd leave any other little diversions, jaunts up to John.

The first round, in May would be in Holland, Hengelo

in the eastern Twente region, to be precise. I doubted we'd have any supernatural duties until we arrived at the more central European rounds, Czech Republic, Germany.

However, we couldn't just pick and choose, we had to be disciplined, keep our cover. We'd also have made a commitment to the Rials and our word is our bond... James Bond... sorry, that slipped out.

Anyway, who was I to say whether we would encounter some being in Holland, Belgium, wherever? Some pesky foe, maybe a lead or vital snippet of information might present itself in the most unlikely of places.

Whilst I was going around in circles, ifs, buts, maybes until the cows came home, John was reading up on Motorsport photography. I'd bought him a decent camera. I don't suppose he could have conjured one up, could he? It would have had to come from somewhere, at someone's expense, so may as well be at mine, albeit second hand.

We'd soon see his research put into practice in a few days, twelve days, come on!

Spring had arrived, well technically. There were a few daffodils dotted about. I was surprised they hadn't drowned or grown flippers, webbed roots!

What had arrived, without doubt, was the Bob Smith Spring Cup race meeting at Oliver's Mount. Lo and behold, the sun was out. I'm not paranoid, who said that? But Mother Nature often played a cruel trick when racing was due up at the Mount. The day before, sunny, the day after sunnier, in-between, well, rainfall of biblical proportions, arks being prepared, animals being sorted into pairs. Maybe she doesn't like all the noise. I say paranoid, but it rarely doesn't rain, somewhere, at some point in time on this, our sceptred isle.

Anyway, it was sunny. Hip, hip, hip hooray!

We set off from Lisa's house, destination, Oliver's Mount. Me in my usual race fan clobber, John in what I presume was his idea of what a sports photographer might wear. Oh, I forgot to mention, John had taken on a new form, new to me anyway. He was a slightly rotund, middle aged, bearded fellow. Ruddy cheeks, bespectacled, sharp eyes which hinted at a serious nature, matching trident laughter lines that contradicted the previous impression.

Rotund may be off the mark. Barrel-chested, wicket keeper's forearms. You could have a beer with this one, an interesting conversation, though you'd be wise to avoid talk of arm-wrestling and the like.

"Why aren't we going up in the van?" asked John.

A question said out loud, but not requiring an answer.

It wasn't that he was weary. It was only a couple of miles. It was just a bit of a dull old trek down Seamer Road. You never seem to be getting anywhere: a road to nowhere. Until you arrive at the Mere, that is. From there, you could see the bikes flying down towards Jefferies Jumps, the anticipation palpable. I think even John, with all his worldly, off-worldly experience, was affected. A definite spring in his step, almost feline!

We cut through the Mere, waterfowl and anglers alike seemingly oblivious to the roaring of motorbikes haring about a few hundred metres up the hill. A quick chat with Duncan and Christine on the gate and we had our digital tickets scanned, wristbands attached.

"The Rials?"

"Patience, my child!" was my response.

"Hurrumph!" John was regressing to disgruntled teenager mode.

All business this one, I thought to myself... have a little patience, Mr Willis.

We had a mooch round the paddock. It was my usual routine. I love the pits, the hub of the event, meeting up with people you only see a couple of times a year, easing seamlessly into previous discussions, like the time in-between never existed.

We wandered about, looking at the various awnings, mechanics making last minute adjustments, riders excitedly discussing some near miss or apologising to a rival for an over-zealous manoeuvre, the soundtrack a mixture of the commentators chatting over the antiquated PA, bikes warming up, announcements booming out to keep the disorderly in order: 'Attention Paddock! Attention Paddock! Supertwins…' A type of bike, not identical caped crusaders, with their underpants over their leggings. 'Please make your way to the holding bay'.

I had to drag John away as he stalked the 'toggers', that's photographers to you and I. Always seemed a bit derogatory that abbreviation. In my opinion, it sounded similar to troglodyte, just my mind doing its usual thing, over-thinking! The 'toggers' didn't seem to mind, no facial spasms evident whenever I'd used the term within earshot or in their company. John was seemingly attracted magnetically to anyone adorned in a white media vest, zig-zagging back and forth, side to side, observing their behaviour. I reiterate, all business.

"Come on, John, the Rials."

A nod of agreement and we headed off up the aptly nicknamed 'Heart Attack Hill'. No problem for John, although he was in full method acting mode, immersed in this new creation, huffing and puffing, stopping two or three times, feigning an interest in some fallen tree limb, watching the bikes charging up Quarry Hill, mimicking those surrounding us, also catching their breath trying to disguise the need, yours truly included.

We arrived at the top. No need to hire a friendly sherpa! Knowing looks from those descending, heading down to the paddock. Well, no need, Smug McSmuggy! You'll be gasping for air yourself, later!

In front of us, football and rugby fields temporarily hosted cars, tents and motor homes. To the left a makeshift avenue of stalls, like the motorcycle version of main street in the wild west. And as I imagine those streets were a hive of activity and excited murmuring, so this was too, no ghost town, no tumbleweeds.

A plethora of food and beverage concerns, merchandise tents, and overshadowing the lot, the behemoth that was the beer tent. Billy Smart's circus or tabletop mountain came to mind.

John spotted the Road Racing News awning and I was sure he quickened the pace. It was refreshing that such a being could still get excited, passionate about things. I mean, he had to be at least five hundred years old, didn't he? I sensed a mental smirk.

Well! I don't know where I got that figure from, the point is, he was aged not jaded.

We sauntered up to the opening of the RRN awning, casual like, and waited for Debra to deal with a customer or two.

"Hello Joel." Welcoming voice, twinkling eyes.

"Hi Debra!"

This was followed by a couple of minutes of high-octane chat, then snap! I jolted. I'd not yet introduced John. I was always doing that, apologies to any previous victims of my unintentional ignorance.

I introduced my friends to each other, then explained a little of our plan as I wasn't sure if Steve had filled Debra in on the detail.

Debra was definitely on board, which was good to hear.

"Talking of Steve," I said. "Where is he? Where's Stevie?"

"Oh, they're just up near the esses."

That's an S shaped stretch of track which incidentally was just a stone's throw from where we were gathered.

As if on command, Steve arrived, a bear hug ensued, followed by Stevie, big Steve's son, a shy smile traversing his face.

We entered into the modern-day wigwam for a pow wow. I'd previously explained to John about the Rials, how special I thought they were. It wasn't until they were gathered together, a trinity, that I observed that John was visibly taken aback, overwhelmed, then drawn to them like a moth.

This behaviour was probably only visible to these semi-trained eyes. Get me! I could perceive it mentally, a ripple in the atmosphere, which in turn built an observable physical reaction. Extremely nuanced, but it was as if the first, the mental, decoded the impression of the latter, the physical. Confused? Yeah? Join the club, semi-trained, remember? Let's just say he seemed temporarily startled, off balance, and leave it at that.

Anyway, John got on well with all three and I knew that he agreed with my earlier suggestion that our true mission should remain our own dirty little secret.

Stevie, Steve and Debra were all onboard with our request. We would represent the Road Racing News platform for the 2024 season.

Debra resumed merchandise duties while I chatted with Stevie about my reporting. What was expected of me, when to file my copy and how. What to concentrate on, results, human stories, paddock gossip etc. Meanwhile John and Steve were hunkered down in deep conversation, discussing shutter speeds, lens sizes. I don't know, I'm paraphrasing. Yes, alright! Making it up. I wasn't really listening. Suffice to say, it was 'togger' talk.

I bought a couple of bits and bobs from Debra, then we said our goodbyes, although we'd see each other again over the weekend. More our formal business discussion farewells.

And so, John and I headed off up towards the bridge over the esses, destination Drury's, a favourite section of mine.

A tea for me, hot chocolate for John and we leant on the wooden barrier, watching the racing, mouth corner talking.

"Do you sense him?" asked John.

"Who?"

"The Deer Man, sorry, Trevor," grinned John.

"No, not yet," I replied.

"I do. It's faint, but he's around. Probably keeping the deer calm, away from the track."

"Why faint though?"

"Cloaking himself, there's a bit of interference in the ether, spiritual," explained John.

"The Rials?"

John nodded, then commented mentally, 'Very strange sensation, pleasant, caught me off guard for an instant. You noticed though, didn't you? Very impressive, Whiskers.'

Back to mouth corner talking again.

"So, what next, Whiskers?"

"Hot-dog, pint? Enjoy the weekend, then put things in place for our trip, destination Holland."

"Sounds like a plan," agreed John Willis. "Whose round is it?"

"You get the dogs, I'll get the beers."

We had a pint and a bite to eat and headed off in opposite directions. John to practise his lensmanship, me meandering from one part of the circuit to another. I reached out to John in the late afternoon and told him I was heading home, second home, the Traf.

His mental reply was short and sweet: 'Enjoy your thimbles,' my code for a couple of quiet, wind down pints, usually a party of one. He gets me.

CONTINENTAL CIRCUS, HENGELO

There were four weeks until the Hengelo meeting, our debut Road Racing News assignment. We'd kept in contact, but for the most part, I did my thing and John, his, whatever his thing was. I didn't ask, we were like most bloke pals. No wasted words, enjoy the comfortable silence, break the fast only to discuss the big things. What was the best brown sauce for example, HP or Daddies? HP of course, no competition.

"How are we getting there? Plane, train, automobile… trans dimensional portal?" I asked John.

"Ferry."

Ooh, nice! I thought, love a good ferry journey.

There was a week to go and I'd started pacing, mentally. I liked to know what's what.

John didn't want any shortcuts, portal wise. He also thought it would be better if he travelled in a conventional way, keeping up appearances, no supernatural trickery.

He'd acquired a valid passport. I don't know, didn't want to know how he'd got hold of it, how kosher it was.

Ferry booked, train timetables studied, we were all set, travelling light, as was my wont. 'Plenty shops sell bread'. That was just a favourite saying of mine. In a nutshell it means don't take the kitchen sink on your travels: other countries also have these things called shops!

I'd picked that saying up in Derby as a twenty something. I lived in Cheltenham at the time and had pals at University in Derby and Nottingham. My mate who was based at RAF Brize Norton would pick me up on Friday and we'd head up the M5 for a weekend of what young-uns did in the early 1990s.

I'd gone into this shop in Derby for some 'Full English' supplies. I asked the Asian shop keeper where the bread was, couldn't find any, either not there or temporarily blinded by the previous night's festivities.

He'd looked at me with a hint of annoyance.

"Plenty shops sell bread!"

Alrighty then, LOL!

It was Friday afternoon and we were on a track, both figuratively and literally. The 15:02 to Hull signalled the beginning of our European adventure. I mentioned earlier how Donald, the shady fellow in the Blacksmith Arms had set us on a track.

That's what John Le Carré calls it, anyway. It's when you're on the hunt for information, you think you know what you're looking for and once satisfied you'll have reached your goal, task completed. Before you know it though, you're on a track, where one query answered quickly leads to another question. You have to be careful though, not get blinkered, inadvertently focused on the next endorphin-inducing discovery, forgetting the task at hand, the goal, the 'Big Boss Battle'!

You'll no doubt have experienced this phenomenon. I shrug my shoulders four times, I'll explain that shortly. Someone asks you what the drummer in some band is called, then you wonder how old he is? Oh, he was married to 'what's her face'. Oh her, her brother was in that film, wonder what year that came out? Now you're on a track! It's two hours later and you've forgotten that drummer's name!

And so, the next journey of discovery commences, leading you down another time sucking black hole. A plague on you, Wikipedia! Back in the day, you'd have given up hours ago, either that or headed off down to the library to search through the reference section. The Encyclopaedia Britannica and the latest Top of the Pops Yearbook forming an unlikely research partnership. Oh, the shoulder shrug thing? It's a trick I developed to help me pronounce words I struggle with. Without it, phenomenon would sound like a 'Brummie' full of cold saying, 'Fuddumidon!'

I raise and lower the shoulders as I work through and pronounce each section of the word in question. Phe – shrug up – nom – shrug down – e – shrug up – nen – shrug down. Try it, it works, it's a laugh if anything!

So yeah, short story long and all that.

We were on a track!

We had to get to Hull and then hop on a bus, destination: the King George dock. Check in for the ferry, the 'Pride of Hull' was seven o'clock in the evening, at the latest, and we'd be underway for half eight.

And in the blink of a very slow eye, we'd be disembarking at Rotterdam around about nine in the morning. It's a long old trek, but there is plenty to do, room to stretch the pins and, well, it's quite refreshing.

No rushing around, time to just enjoy the journey, not a headless chicken in sight.

For now though, we were land bound, train-travelling. A much shorter journey: about an hour and twenty. It does seem to drag though, when you're confined to your chair and assigned table portion. Not that you can't get up, move about. But where to go? This isn't a Poirot novel, no murders, hopefully. No dimly lit corridors, posh dining cars and the like. Besides, I always lose my balance traversing the aisles on a train, like a drunkard feigning sobriety.

It's on such rare occasions as these that I tend to break the silence, seeking a bit of chat to pass the time.

"You prefer train travel… why is that, John?"

"You get time to see the scenery, animals, people at work. An honest, on the surface anyway, window into how things should be," was my friend's considered reply.

"Ferries too?"

"Well, for the most part all you see, pardon the pun, is great big dirty lumps of greyish water. In the North Sea anyway."

"I bet you can see beyond, within a body of water though? The sea-life, gold doubloon-laden wrecks adorning the seabed?"

"You're such a romantic, Whiskers! Anyway, sounds a bit voyeuristic, pervy!"

Well, that was my need for conversation sated. I descended into the comfort of my reverie, aka talking to myself, in my own head, you understand.

I like trains, train-travel. Well, the thought of it,

the romance of travel. Not quite the same in reality, especially now that I can hear thoughts too. The inane jibber jabber, business men in cheap suits, iPads, talking on the phone about networking, blue sky thinking, you know, drivel: stating the obvious 'I'm on the train, we're pulling into the station now' while waving at the other party, through the window.

Funnily enough, we were, pulling into Hull station. I forced myself not to mention the fact to John, given my previous rant.

It really felt like the adventure had started. Here, now. How did I feel? Excited, yes! Trepidatious too, is that even a word? Fact-check, yes. Thank you, Google.

With a spring in my step, John playing it cool, sauntering, we headed off to find our bus, the five o'clock. Forty minutes to pass, I fell into step with John. He raised an eyebrow, Roger Moore style. A sheepish grin from me... bah!

We boarded the Pride of Hull and I led the way, John's turn to follow in my wake. No cabin for us, not that I'm tight, it just didn't seem worth it. Unless you planned on hooking up, or throwing up over the next dozen hours. We booked in and I was informed that we actually did have a cabin.

Apparently, it was non-negotiable on this route. Gone are the days when the bar couches and ledges were festooned with people sleeping off the previous night's festivities. Anyway, it was included in the booking so no worries, somewhere to sling our gear.

I did my usual ferry thing. I don't get sea sick, just a bit disoriented. Something to do with the harmonics makes me feel a bit wobbly, confused.

First stop, the buffet restaurant. It was a bit expensive, but always tasty. Anyway, you're a captive audience, so tasty trumps cost. Besides it wasn't like Just Eat delivered by jet-ski... did they?

Something substantial was the order of the day, on this occasion: fish, chips, beans, bread and butter, and a pot of tea. John had gone all continental on me: croissant and coffee. Didn't really go with his attire or current form, for that matter. He reminded me of Raymond Briggs's Father Christmas. When he goes on holiday to France.

I was chuckling away to myself when to my alarm, I received a flash image of Father Christmas having a rough night after overindulging on the food and wine.

It wasn't me laughing now! I really had to work harder to conceal my thoughts. John Blooming Willis!

The second stage of my highly developed ferry strategy was to mooch around the shops, avoiding all the expensive, fragrant items and instead selecting some reading material, preferably inexpensive. Not tight though, remember?

John picked up a photography magazine, me a copy of Classic Racer and we headed off to find the most appropriate watering hole. We settled on the Irish Bar. Seemed apt for a couple of road racing journo types. Not for us the show bar or brasserie, I don't do cocktails or wine. I'd decided to avoid the lounge bar on this occasion. The last time I found myself in there, I strong armed the pianist into accompanying me and my mates while we performed a shouty, slurry rendition of 'Ebony and Ivory'.

We had a few beverages then went to stretch our legs on the ironically named sun deck, although to be fair, it, the sun, had been a bit more outgoing recently.

A few pints always does the trick for me, gives me my sea legs. Alcohol has the opposite effect in ferry world. The reverse stagger effect. You've seen people staggering down the street after a few pints mixed with some fresh air. Well, the opposite is true at sea. You stagger about a bit, pre-drinks, as the ship rolls on the waves, then as you become more, let's say relaxed, the reverse stagger reveals itself.

Passenger 1. 'The state of it, must be absolutely trollied!'

Passenger 2. 'What makes you say that?'

Passenger 1. 'No stagger, innit!'

Passenger 2. 'Aye, an utter disgrace!'

Passenger 1. 'Pint?'

Passenger 2. 'You've twisted my arm, grab that railing, you're all over the place.'

We decided to catch a late film, well, the nine o'clock screening to be exact. I'm not much of a film buff, but as long as the Dolby was reasonable, I could always take forty winks.

I opted for the new Bob Marley film. Music, yes, but I presumed there wouldn't be a great deal of explosions and shouty stuff. He was a pretty laid-back chilled fellow, after all.

John Willis chose Kung Fu Panda 4. Yeah, I know. Ours is not to reason why.

A perfect Whiskers journey if I do say so myself. I made sure I was out on deck first thing, the sun still stretching and rising seemingly from its water bed. I'd polished off a bacon buttie and stood with tea in one hand, woodbine in the other.

Just gazing and breathing in the fresh air, in between inhalations of Virginian tobacco, watching on as Rotterdam port came into view and welcomed us in.

Time to test our 'land legs'.

Train time again, well, after a short tram journey to Rotterdam 'Centraal Station'.

"Remind me, why didn't we just use a portal again? Hurrumph!"

No reaction from John, I suppose you had to have a more developed level of patience when you reached a certain age. Have a greater understanding of time.

By the time I'd finished grumbling to myself, we were seated on the train to Hengelo. I don't know what all the fuss was about. Got to have a moan now and again though, it's tradition.

Another train then, albeit a cleaner, more modern version. Public transport, roads, they all seemed so much tidier on the continent. Bit of a sweeping statement, pardon the pun. Maybe this rather naïve view would come crashing down to the ground in the weeks that followed. Only time would tell.

The penultimate leg of this particular journey completed, we emerged bleary-eyed from Hengelo station. We quickly located the taxi rank and set off on the short drive to the circuit.

We were initially going to spend the weekend in Hengelo proper, at the Hotel Drachten or the City Hotel Hengelo, both reasonable, price-wise. But John reckoned it would be more in keeping and practical if we bedded down in the paddock.

So, tent it was. Steve Rial had pulled some strings for us and pleasingly and most appreciated, everything was set up for us when we arrived. Hotel Willis-Whiskers was a large blue tent, with screen porch. Inside, two cots, table and chairs, camping lantern and welcome hamper. Get us! I could get used to this.

I can sleep anywhere, apart from on trains, planes and ferries. Hmmm, the point being, I didn't need a King-sized bed, and all that jazz. I could sleep on a twiglet!

John Willis? I imagined he was of the same ilk. But maybe he used astral projection, transcendental something or other. Projected himself into his home, if he had one, or some five-star hotel.

I doubted it though, kind of a wherever I lay my hat type of entity was our Mr Willis.

The track, well, to be accurate, the road, public, lay three miles out of Hengelo proper. On Friday night, the riders set off from the paddock and gathered in the town centre for a meet and greet. It felt out of the ordinary, almost naughty. Was this allowed these days? And that was before the racing had even started. There were fleeting moments when you questioned whether it was real, watching racing on public roads. Home of the family saloon, bus, white van, one minute: the next full-on race track.

Hengelo, my kind of town! Sorry, Telly Savalas moment there, but in this case, it happened to be true. If you don't know what I'm on about, check out his travelogue about Birmingham.

We had a great night, John taking the odd picture, me just chatting with the 'odd' person. Still not picking up on anything out of the ordinary, so I relaxed and just soaked up the atmosphere. A buzz in the air, young and old enjoying the opportunity to chat with the racers, away from the more serious vibe that descends once racing commences. Happy people, nice bikes and sidecar outfits. The beer relaxed the mood further, the wafting aroma of hotdogs igniting audible hunger pangs. Stomach appeased, then the throat cried out for more thirst-quenching liquid. And so, the night went on, until people and machinery drifted away. Long day tomorrow for all involved.

We declined a lift back on some Heath Robinson inspired sidecar combination. I'd have gone for it, but despite it being three miles, I wanted to stretch my legs.

John concurred and we strode off into the moonlit night. All was quiet now, just the night music, nature's soundtrack. Things you only heard once those noisy humans shut their traps and settled in for the night.

It was an opportune moment for me to exercise mine, do what I do best, most. Ask questions.

"So, when did you first start watching over me? If that's what you did."

"Since before your birth…" This latest revelation accompanied by a development of the previously used Marx Brother's eyebrow wiggle. A spooky finger waggling component added for extra effect… "Hamish."

"Hamish?"

"Your Dad was going to name you that, until a whisper in your mother's ear pardoned you that ignominy. Imagine a growing lad with a service brat accent trying to pull that off! A tall order even with your legendary cheek. I left you alone in Cyprus as you seemed at your happiest. Any time you went off the rails, veered off the path straight and true, I guided you, pulled strings, but don't get me wrong, sometimes hard lessons needed to be learnt."

"And what about the strange experiences I've had? The colourful orbs that surrounded my bed as a child, the frightening dream of a woodsman, axe in hand, attacking Dad. Those two are the oldest memories I can still recall, vividly. One comforting, the other frightening. I obviously never got them from watching TV, at the age of four. Besides only a couple of channels, one television per household back then."

"That was regular Angels and demons, monitoring your development, observing. Assessing you as a potential tool for either good or bad."

"The wing type marking on my shoulder blade?" I asked.

"A marker, beacon of sorts."

"The scratches?" Three scratches that appeared on my lower back in my mid-twenties after a disturbing interaction with some type of entity. I was pretty sure I knew the answers to these questions. Confirmation is always comforting though.

"A regular demonic, shadow man."

"Talking of which, the shadows swirling round the bed?"

"That was xenos surrounding you. You resolved that yourself. Reached out to the Society for Psychical Research. They helped you."

"So, you've always been there, for me?"

John nodded. A grin started to form.

"To put it bluntly, you're my pet project."

Curiosity satisfied, for now. We strode forth once more.

The circuit's resident windmill came into view, surrounded by a myriad of twinkling lights, lamps hanging from tents and awnings. No noisy generators were allowed at this time of night.

I'd say they appeared on the horizon, but that's a moot point. Everything is tied to the horizon in this neck of the woods. It's so flat, you see.

Tent located, we settled in. It had been a long day and I was ready for a dream or three. John Willis reverted to his favoured feline form. I raised a mental eyebrow. John answered my unspoken query.

"I prefer it, I feel cosy, aloof, limber, flexible."

"A handsome devi... cough... specimen too!"

"I'm aware." A wry grin emanated from Mr Willis.

We didn't encounter anything out of the ordinary in Hengelo. I wasn't complaining, mind. That was a good thing. Cover intact, roles established. We were free to enjoy the occasion, fulfil our RRN tasks, bond some more.

I'm not saying we hadn't gone unnoticed. For all I knew, they were observing us via a crystal ball or green liquid-filled cauldron. John didn't seem perturbed. Besides, he'd thrown himself headlong into his new role, character, 'Togger' extraordinaire, sausage eating, beer swilling, road racing fanatic.

"You really do enjoy the bikes, don't you, John?"

"Oh yes!" A few octaves higher than the norm, promptly over-corrected. Now a rumbling baritone. "So many facets, excitement, bravery, a test of self, new tech. The Achille's heel: cost, money, dosh."

"Yes, a bit of a difference from the usual fatherly sporting encouragement: a pair of footy boots or a shiny new golf bat…"

I was cut off by an infamous John Willis furrowed brow.

"Golf club," I corrected myself. He liked things on the nose, as it were. Especially when we were discussing grown up stuff, philosophy and the like.

"It's no coincidence, my penchant for race circuits. We all need a passion, Whiskers. Good for the soul."

"If you have one!"

A snort was John's dignified reply to that one.

So that was Hengelo. We packed up. Didn't take long. We travelled light: no tent, no living accoutrements. Just a rucksack each, remember. "Plenty shops sell bread!"

I filed my report, or was it copy? Whatever, I won't

bore you with the details. Needless to say, it was awesome! John's images were top notch, by the way. Next stop for the intrepid reporters, slash spies, spooks? Or whatever we were: Germany.

SAUSAGE SCHLEIZ

John Willis

John here, reflecting on Schleizer Dreieck, in Germany. About time I talked to you again, heard things from my perspective. Whiskers? He's under the weather. Strange saying, isn't it? We're all under the weather, aren't we?

Whiskers often puts me on a pedestal, but I'm as fallible as the next... 'being'. Not omnipotent me. I imagined, incidentally a powerful if not foolproof tool, that Germany was just another leg on our IRRC journey, a Road Racing News commitment.

Oh boy! Was I wrong. Yes, I was aware of some of the myths and tales associated within the general area of Thuringia. I wasn't sure of what was folklore and what was reality. I'd know once I set foot or paw on German soil, got into range. I could have tuned in beforehand, but where's the fun, the adventure in that?

What unfolded was a major development. These revelations would see us closing in on the focus of our quest. Whiskers may not have been on the ground, but in the weeks that followed he would refine his abilities, grow in stature and confidence.

I fully expected Whiskers to cope valiantly with his reporting, from afar. Thanks to me of course, sending him the 'gen', via my mind.

So here was I, in Schleiz. As alluded to earlier, Whiskers was unwell, I was alone. I thought I'd welcome a bit of solo sleuthing. However, I missed the constant questions, naive exuberance, the company.

He had one of those 'humany' type afflictions. I won't go into detail, mentor-mentee confidentiality and all that. Suffice to say, it wasn't life threatening. Neither was it inconsequential. You humans really ought to do away with all that butchers-esque plumbing and gooey jiggery-pokery. About time you evolved. You'd be better off and far less gross!

Brucie bonus! No need for all those medical dramas, stomach – if I had one – churning reality shows. Operating on this, removing that. Yuk! I mean it's morbid at best, perverse at worst. Anyway, I digress… he was poorly.

I'd taken the pictures, passed the race results and bits of gossip onto Whiskers. He'd managed to piece everything together and with the help of other reports from social media, produced a great report. I was pleased with my images and all in all had a great time around the paddock.

I was being spied upon, but I didn't let it spoil my weekend. I'd deal with this interloper in my own good time. In the meantime, I had some sleuthing to do. I'd also noticed another unworldly force in the area, this one more benevolent. No soft touch, but not what I would class as an enemy.

It's difficult to explain unless you've experienced this sort of contact before. It was nothing as in your face as a voicemail or note popped through your letterbox. It was more like an impulse to set off in a certain direction, not siren song-like in strength. More of a gentle invite: your choice whether to accept.

I chose to accept. Any knowledge was useful to me and I was intrigued. There aren't many beings who have access to this talent, this network, if you like. Besides, it had emanated from close by, the general Thuringia area.

So, I let Whiskers know what I was up to. No specifics. Didn't exactly know myself. I just told him I'd catch up later, back in Scarborough.

Woe is me! I had to hop on a train. Well, you know by now that I don't have any need to rely on traditional forms of public transport. It's just my not so guilty pleasure.

Anybody who's experienced a cancelled train or missed a connecting flight would tear your arm off for the ability to portal here or there. I understand that, but to me, at my age, I enjoy the bit in-between. I like the journey, the interactions, people watching. I can zone out in case of delay, ponder, soak up the atmosphere.

My destination was the Rennsteig, a popular 'ridge walk' that runs through the Thuringian Forest. More a trek than a walk, mind: it's over a hundred miles in length.

I hopped on the bus at Schleiz. The next leg of this unnecessary journey would be Stadtroda where I'd board my train for Erfut. I'd decided to stop over there for the night then catch the train to Rennsteig in the morning. See? I don't need a hotel, a train... all that jazz. It's just my bag. It's fun. Just me, myself and I. Gazing out of a glazed rectangle, watching an ever-changing landscape portrait, sitting in a hotel bar watching the world go by. Me likey! Up bright and early, continental breakfast consumed. I headed out, no feline form for this ramble. Mid-thirties, slim, generic European look. Sturdy walking attire, but still refined, not looking out of place in the rather nice hotel lobby. Hotel Kaiserhof Eisenach, such a beautiful language is German, not shouty at all...

He didn't approach me until I'd been walking for about forty minutes. He'd picked up on my mental 'Do Not Disturb' sign. I wanted to enjoy the morning, the sights and smells, get accustomed to my surroundings. So, I walked, trekked, whatever you call it.

I came to a halt near a clearing in the forest, dropped my veil, so to speak, and waited for my host to appear.

"Ah, Ruby! I had an inkling it would be you."

"Don't be coy, John Willis, you knew very well who was 'calling'."

"Well, this means of communication is lacking in caller-id. Why the subterfuge?"

"I have my reputation to think of, John, besides there are other unworldly creatures roaming this place. Best to keep them guessing, if just for the sport."

"I didn't realise Thuringia was your neck of the woods, the forest?"

"All are in my neck, as you term it, Mr Willis. Close enough anyway, young Whopper Snipper!"

I forgave him that: probably only speaks English on the rare occasion, not forgetting he's easily upset.

Oh, how rude of me! I'd best give you the lowdown

on this Ruby, this um… acquaintance of mine. You may know him as Rübezahl, although he's not too fond of that particular moniker.

Rubez… Ruby is a mythical creature made real. He is prominent in folklore, not only here where we both stood, but in those countries that share a border with what we think of as modern Germany. Don't forget that these continental countries are always squabbling; the boundaries change, but the people don't, so you have enclaves of German speakers on either side of a line on the map.

That's another thing, folklore… some think these tales stem from the fantasies, fears and other made-up nonsenses from a bunch of unwashed jelly brains. A lot of jibber jabber spouting from the mouths of dim-witted peasants from a past best forgotten.

Well, that couldn't be further from the truth. Simply put, it's a collection of stories, beliefs and such. Passed down through the generations by word of mouth. Obviously, some part of these tales will be nonsense to scare the kids, make them behave. Some will have been embellished, but many are based in absolute truth. Ruby, being a case in point. I mean, I can smell him from here! Only joking. Smells quite nice, pine needles or some such.

Back to Ruby. He's a mountain spirit, self-proclaimed Lord of the Mountains, a bit unpredictable at times, not unlike the weather that he's able to control.

His dislike of his full name? Oh, it's to do with some lass, princess if I recall, very messy. Something to do with turnips, don't ask! Come to think of it, maybe I should stop calling him Ruby? I mean Rübe is German for turnip… isn't it? Ah, na! I'm sure he'll let me know one way or the other.

In other stories, he's depicted as a friendly giant albeit with a wrathful side, if you disrespect him that is. There are loads of traits associated with old Rubes. Mind you, we each change over time, and it's all about first impressions. If you're grouchy on a morning, that doesn't necessarily mean you're a misery in the evening.

Some describe him as gnome-like, others as a giant. He does have the same shape-shifting gift I have, which may explain that away. I've only encountered him on a couple of occasions, but I like him. Maybe the feeling is mutual? He can be mischievous at times, good fun, for the most part. He's pretty generous with his time and knowledge. Don't treat him for a fool, mind, no one likes that and underneath this calm exterior, lies an extremely powerful being.

Oh, by the way he was currently in the form of a majestic black bear. I don't know if they're native to this place. I doubt he bothers about such details.

Ruby cleared his throat and began to talk. Well, I listened, of course. Big furry bear for one, impressive, cuddly. I was genuinely interested to hear what he had to say. I had no idea, can't read this one's mind. It would be impolite, not the done thing in these circles.

"I like balance," Ruby said. "I've grown fond of these unruly children, my wards. I don't appreciate these dullards. Meddling and conniving in my affairs. What is it with these dudes, John Willis? What's their motivation? I may be old, wise… powerful. But this political scene, it's not mine. I like nature, understand it: furry, growly things, trees, babbling brooks. I suppose I've mellowed over time. Bit of an old hippy these days." Ruby started to boom. "I don't appreciate 'people' coming into my garden, trampling all over it, disrupting the status quo!"

"Hippy maybe, but evidently, this bear still has teeth!" I declared.

"Oh yes! Old habits die hard."

A sparkle in his eyes, tensed shoulders, release and relax, a self-conscious lop-sided grin emerged. The message? Don't mess with this born-again nature lover. He'll bite hard! If poked.

"You young…" he began.

I raised an eyebrow.

"…energetic types need to fight the good fight. Are you young, John Willis? Relatively speaking?"

Silence. I broke it with a shrug.

"Nevertheless, you are the man…" He paused, brow furrowing. "…for the job. And I have some info that might aid you in this task. Whether you are aware or not, I don't know, but I shall tell you anyway." He raised his arms in the air, fists clenched, and announced, "Bulgaria!"

"Bulgaria?"

"Yes, that's where you need to go if you want to root out the thing, the mastermind behind all this disturbance…"

"In the force?"

Ruby roared, not in anger. Laughter.

"Yes, you could be right, John. Anyway, these alien pests are bugging me…"

"And I need to get the bug repellent and banish this head honcho. Restore order, preserve that balance that you crave?" I suggested.

"Correct, John. These are my forests and I'll be damned if I'll allow these aliens to sow seeds of dissent just so they can, can… I don't know what they want with this place. Destroy it? Turn it into some fun park? I don't care and I won't allow it. I mean, some of them have been here for thousands of years. What's with these new guys? I can't stomach all this conniving and scheming."

"I now have my focus, locus, my nemesis, Ruby, that's the important thing and I'm grateful that you reached out to me. However, we mustn't forget that the majority of these aliens, for want of a better word, are what I'd term as friendly in this context. They share a lot of traits with humanity, admittedly, not the best ones. They're interested in business and profit, that's a two-way street and they would much prefer to work with humanity, not against it. It's this xenophobe lot that we're dealing with, intent on destroying the harmony and balance you crave, Ruby. Why? Because they can't stand humans, anyone different. They barely tolerate each other. Just another galactic infestation to purge. They aren't interested in this planet, they'll most likely abandon it, move onto the next genocide on their list. Who knows what they'll do with Earth once they've achieved their goal. Leave it, destroy it. I doubt they even know themselves, or care."

"You need to fix this, John."

"Oh, I will, Ruby, one way or the other. But for now, I have an uninvited guest keeping tabs on me."

"Ha! Happy hunting, my friend!"

I knew very well who'd sent this chap. He was here to observe, kept his distance, trying to merge into the crowd. Not bad tradecraft but no match for someone with my gifts. On observing him, I'd had a sneaky peak inside his mind. No harm to him and as a standard human, he was oblivious. I'd let Whiskers deal with this ignoramus. Hell! I'd let him deal with his master too.

When he, they, got nothing from me, they'd go after the supposed weakest link, Whiskers.

Well, they'd be in for a shock. My protégé was anything but weak. Even he didn't realise how strong he'd become. I'd not leave him high and dry though. I'd get the popcorn and watch the action from afar.

THE OPPOSITION

'Who are you?' I could sense him, creeping around, probing my mind for a weakness in my defences.

I'd missed the trip to Schleiz, not feeling 100% and then this intrusion started. Maybe it had been going on for a while, unnoticed, drowned out by the day-to-day noises of life.

I'd been in bed for a couple of days. No TV, no radio warbling in the background. Just my thoughts and the odd medley of birdsong. Several types at once, an avian re-mix in 'da house'.

And with this quietude came a focus. Nothing else to do. I noticed this benign attack and sought advice from John. He didn't seem unduly worried. Emboldened, I confronted this cheeky little intruder.

'Who are you?!'

This time with a more forceful thrust of mental energy. The trespasser was clearly alarmed by this demand for information, but gathered his composure relatively quickly.

'My name? Gurpslin Lindt. No! It has nothing to do with those stupid chocolate rabbits! Humans! Why do you always have to seek connections, words, images. Oooh, that cloud looks like my Grandma… funny looking lady she must have been. It's ridiculous, you're all so… so…. so rudimentary! I do like their crest though. A dragon, very impressive. Krasnak! You've got me doing it now. I've been on this planet, this floating dung ball, for far too long! Anyway, back to my name. Roughly translated into your slimy, sickening tongue it means 'functionary'... cough... ahem... 'petty functionary'. However, I'm a lot more than the sum of those words, parts? I'm getting confused now, it's this disgusting, gritty air, dust, everything!'

Confused, eh?

Let's see what more we can learn, what I can anyway... we have his name for starters. Revealing it was either a slip of the tongue or intentional. He's either an idiot, most likely or it's a cover name. Maybe they don't bother with all the spy, tradecraft stuff or it's a part of this xenophobic disdain for anything other. To circle back, I go with the idiot option. I was sure John had the measure of this, creature? Let's just refer to him in the masculine for now.

'Where are you from?'

'Let's just say I'm not a native of this place, this so-called planet. Suffice to say, I'm not from this neck of the woods.'

'Yet, you have a good grasp of the vernacular for a non-resident?'

'It's not exactly difficult, hardly complex, this primitive lingo of yours, is it?'

'Oh, come on Mr Lindt. Can I call you Bunny?'

'No, you may not! Stop this insolence! I know what your...'

I cut him off. 'Okay, okay, but seeing as you've invaded my privacy, let yourself into my mental mansion...'

He returned the favour! 'Hardly a grand one...'

'Alright, so it's decided, Bunny it is. I'm glad we've cleared that up.'

'But, now I never…'

Anyway, I was about to say. You must have some device, some cheat. Notwithstanding the lack of complexity. I very much doubt you picked up this alien to you language in a heartbeat. Do you have a heart, internal organs, a soul?'

'Whiskers! Yes, now I understand! Annoying little biped, aren't you?'

Biped, hey, he must be less or more 'pedal' than the average bear. This is fun, I thought. I should invite him back some time.

'To answer your question, accusation, I, like you, have this thing that you so eloquently refer to as a brain. You should try using it sometime. I happen to have a fluency in many of your planet's languages and a fair few dialects too… ya ken?' Lindt chuckled.

I presumed that's what he was doing, either that or gargling coal.

Whatever the noise indicated, it sounded uncomfortable, made me swallow involuntarily as I wished I had a cough sweet at hand.

'I'm sharing your mindspace now, remember? However, you seem to have developed yours, I can't quite waltz through all your nooks and crannies. Normally I can just access all areas of your brethren's tiny brains, pick up the local colloquialisms, master the language, a simple task for I!'

'Hardly an achievement then, being so simple. So,

what exactly are you up to? What's the reasoning behind this unwanted attention?'

'The reason? The reason?'

"Yes, yes!"

'I'm the opposition, to you! To that holier than thou companion of yours, Mr John 'goody two shoes' Willis, or whatever he's calling himself lately. Slinking around um… um… drinking milk, licking his paws. Or stumbling around Holland, sweating and panting, taking his pathetic pictures, hamming it up, masquerading! And, Mr Whiskers, my job is to fix things, annoying things, to fix you; to pour misery on the lot of you. Anything I can do to make your lives miserable is a victory. I know what that talking furball is up to, a damn sight more than you do! In short, Mr Whiskers, I intend to lead you to your inevitable doom. Oh, I'm sure he will be alright, he always is. But, you! You're another matter. I'm going to thwart you, divert you, deceive you. This adventure you're embarked upon will fail, and if I can't ensure that this human race of yours disappears, I'll guarantee that you, Mr Whiskers, you will fall!'

'What's up, Doc? Get out of the wrong side of bed this morning?'

'Wha… I don't understand this reference. Who is this Doc?'

'No matter, have a carrot, it'll make you feel better, see past your confusion, shed light on the matter.'

'Carrot? Doc? What are you saying? You filthy creatures infuriate me!'

"This bloke really is an idiot. Simple is definitely the

word." Did I say that out loud? Oh dear, did I mean to? Oh yes! Hee, hee.

'I heard that!'

'My apologies, Bunny. Thank you for all the information, don't leave the door open on your way out.'

'What information?'

'Oh damn! Did I say that out loud? Stop confusing me, you insolent piece of…'

I slammed the door, my mind, shut.

So, that was Bunny then, the opposition. Well, if that was the standard of the intellects we were facing, I wasn't going to lose any sleep.

However, best not to underestimate your opponent. Stupidity doesn't necessarily negate power. I mean, look around you. This thing, well, he was some type of rabbity thing in my imagination. He could still pose a real danger, to me. He was right, there. I'll give him that. Of Flesh and Bone am I, or whatever they say. I may not know all the sayings, but I'm smart enough to realise my fallibility… or is it my vulnerability. Honest, I am smart, quite smart.

I dialled up John, figuratively. See? Smart. I felt confident in the way I'd handled the situation, but I was still a little out of my depth. I needed reassurance, a pat on the head.

'Lindt? Oh, he's a buffoon alright. I had no doubt you'd annoy him. No offence, Whiskers, it's the perfect strategy with the Gurpslin Lindts of this universe.'

'I call him Bunny.'

'Ha, I bet that Bugs him!'

'Nice, I didn't think you'd get that reference, John.'

'Oh, don't worry, Whiskers, I know my onions, not to mention my carrots.'

'So, you know Bunny then. Care to elaborate?'

'Not really.'

'Krasnak! Fair enough, next stop Finland?'

'Indeed.'

SUOMI

The cat was well and truly out of the bag, to pardon the pun. Whether this Bunny character knew a little or a lot was moot, the fact that he knew something meant our cover was blown.

To tell you the truth, I think they, the opposition, were on to John from the very start. Remember the man, Milton? On the bench in Aberdare Park? I'd initially thought he was on the level, victim of an unwanted attachment. Boy, was I wrong.

I was sure word had got back to those who intended to thwart us. Or one of the parties. I was in the dark, for now. I didn't yet know who all the players were in this game of ours. I imagined it was a need-to-know situation. Perhaps John Willis would enlighten me at some point. That was fine by me. I had enough to think about for now. Why clutter up my mind with loads of ifs, buts and maybes.

By the way, I was pretty sure that John had planned all of this from the start, probably before that. Before the start? Well, you know what I mean: prior!

I think he chose Aberdare, knowing that there would be someone there who would go running back to their master or at least spill the beans to someone connected to the 'baddies', whoever they may be.

John most likely wanted to see who and what raised their collective heads above the parapet. Drawing them out into the open, using their interest, their scheming to ultimately expose the location of our foe. A nice piece of subterfuge in my opinion, being thought of as prey, only to turn the tables at an opportune moment. Becoming the hunter, not the hunted.

That was the first point, please be aware, this was just speculation on my part. I could just have confronted John. I doubted he'd give me a straight answer though. It was probably in order to protect me in some way. I was cool with that, ignorance is bliss, 'que sera sera'. The second point was, I reckoned John just liked messing with these forces of darkness. I didn't think he saw them as nemeses, just things to play with, like a cat terrorising a ball of wool.

You know what though? I think he just loved watching the bike racing too, the atmosphere in the paddock. I didn't know who he answered to, or if he even had any masters. I presumed so. Maybe he didn't have any annual leave left this millennium, so was mixing business with pleasure. Was he just on a jolly, getting his racing fix paid for on subsistence? I doubted they'd pay for his mileage though, his train travel fetish. Not with all these portals available to him. With all that being said, it transpired that he really did need me. With my ability to sense the presence of the xenos, I brought light to John's blind-spot.

Anyway, I'm getting off-topic. Back to the point in hand, Finland, and how I dealt with this knowledge. So, our operation had been compromised in some fashion. Seeing as I was only really aware of my next assignment, I didn't have the full picture. Taking that into consideration, I thought it was prudent just to trust in John.

It would have been far too easy to second guess each and every interaction I'd experienced up to this point and from here on in. A trap I wanted to avoid, to step over. I'd be doing their work for them, no need to lead me off on false trails if I was going round in circles off my own back.

However, I couldn't just pretend my 'conversation' with Bunny never took place. So, I'd decided. I'd just go with the flow. If Bunny wanted a rematch, bring it on!

Finland, Imatra bound. The team back together: the dynamic duo! Me back on form, us, the mission, back on track.

We flew out from Leeds Bradford airport, destination: Helsinki via Schiphol in Amsterdam.

John said he would take care of all the arrangements for the trip. Maybe he'd had his fill of trains for the time being, doubt it though.

He'd pulled some strings. I never asked, although I had my theories. Whatever universal vibrations were at play bothered me not.

As I luxuriated in my business class throne, I could only conclude that these were indeed, good vibrations. See what I did there? Physics, music, they're all connected. Bazinga!

I was enjoying this, I could most definitely get used to it. Leg room, who'd have thought? It seems the bigger the plane, the smaller the room allocated for the human cargo. Not like those magazine adverts from the golden age of travel. Anyway, that was then and this is now, enjoy it, you misery!

To snap myself out of this reverie I thought I'd pester John instead, I'm such a generous soul.

"Do you think Bunny will make an appearance, John?" I asked.

"In Finland? Him? Noooo! If anything, he'll dispatch one of his underlings. That slimy little toad thinks he's above all that. No field work for him. Wouldn't want to get his manus dirty."

"Manus?"

John waved his hands at me. "Hands. Bunny has delusions of grandeur, when in reality he's just a..."

"Petty functionary?"

John laughed. "Ha, yes! He's quite far down the food chain, albeit with powerful masters. This overinflated ego of his, that's actually very useful to us. It's a weakness, a fissure. And that provides us with an opportunity. We can poke at that weak point and see what lies beyond. He'll deliver us to our true adversaries at a time of our choosing, all the while thinking he's in control. All hail Bunny evil genius."

"Don't rate him very highly, do you, John?"

"He wears westcuts!"

"Westcuts?" I asked, not quite sure what John was going on about.

"Westcuts, westcuts! It's how I say waistcoats, with a Scottish drawl, it sounds cool, Whiskers! Anyway, if I can make my point?"

"Go on."

"Thank you. People who wear over-colourful, garish… westcuts… are overcompensating. Normally junior management types. Trying to seem cool to their underlings, formal to their higher ups, failing at both. The brighter the westcut, the duller the person."

No argument from me as I offered my two penn'orth. "Only snooker players should wear 'WAISTCOATS' these days, handy little pocket for the chalk and so on."

"Correct."

We passed the next twenty seconds in contemplative, chin nodding silence then returned to our previous activities.

I knew next to nothing about Finland, the Finnish. En tiedä mitään which translates to 'I don't know anything'. I'm not even sure if that's correct. Complicated language, that I do know.

I'd read about the local foods, drinks. You know, the usual touristy things. You pretend to be all cosmopolitan, prepared to try the local delicacies. Truth be told, you're just seeing if they eat anything similar to your grub back home. Hoping they drink your favourite brand of beer. Do they stock HP sauce? You know, the important stuff.

I figured I'd pick that sort of thing up on the fly, so I focused on the history, the culture. As such, I was reading the 'Kalevala', a collection of folk poems, featuring Finnish mythological creatures. Not just any book of poetry this, the Kalevala is held in high regard, often referred to as the 'Finnish national epic'.

Colour me intellectual!

I'd lost my thread, partly me and my wandering mind,

partly the groans and murmurings emanating from the seat next to me.

It was John Willis. Well, it was the device nestled in his palms. A fancy new Steam Deck, John deep in concentration, tongue poking out like a handkerchief from the breast pocket of a... WAISTCOAT.

I peered over, trying not to distract him from the task in hand, smashing zombies' heads in by the looks of it. I recognised the game, '7 days to die'. Good taste, John, I nodded absent-mindedly.

It was funny to think of a powerful being like John Willis playing videogames, this entity whose intellect and wisdom cast a shadow over all that stood before him. I supposed when you've seen, done and know all, it was difficult to entertain yourself. I doubted he found himself wandering about with starry eyes these days. At least with these games, he could ramp up the difficulty level if he needed a challenge, perhaps taste defeat on occasion.

Or perhaps he was just a gamer. That's a universal constant, I reckoned.

I turned back to my book. Where was I?

Maybe John could just gift me this knowledge? But knowing isn't understanding. I should just read, discover for myself...

Perhaps he could gift me the understanding? Oh, just read the blooming thing, lazy sod. No wonder they call me Whiskers. I was annoying myself now. So many questions! Find out yourself! Shut up and read!

I glanced at John, still playing, cleansing 'Navezgane'

of the undead, a smirk forming at the corner of his mouth, spreading like a virus.

Damn! I really needed to work on my discipline, mind-wise.

I read.

And I was glad I did. What an interesting mix of creatures feature in Finnish folklore. They seemed to hold animals and nature in the highest regard. Nice. The bear figured prominently, as bears do. They were seen as sacred spirits and right up there when ranking the strongest forces in nature. You couldn't really argue with that. Nature as in the animal side, I wouldn't pit a bear against a tornado, that wouldn't be fair now, would it?

The Kalevala contained a whole host of mythological creatures, a veritable smorgasbord or to be accurate, Voileipäpöytä of Finnish delights, well, some more delightful than others! I noticed that there were a lot who call the water their home. I was yet to encounter a 'lakey', watery-type being so that could be interesting. I'd give Näkki a miss though, if it was at all possible: sounded like a real jerk! Loved luring children into the water and subsequently drowning them. To think of it, I wouldn't mind crossing swords with him, maybe when John was around though. I say, him, but apparently, Näkki was one of those pesky shapeshifters too. So, God only knows what his original form was.

Come to think of it, he was probably the only one that could explain why this piece of work existed in the first place.

Another thing that stood out, although I didn't know

if it would be of any help to us, was the three souls theory, or was it belief? I don't want to offend anyone. Helpful or not, you know me: curious. Knowledge is power. On the flip-side, ignorance is bliss. I'd go for the former every time, no ostrich me.

Anyway, the three souls.

In Finnish mythology, there are three different parts of the soul: the henki, luonto, and itse. The henki is the soul that we are born with, and it's said that it is the source of life and responsible for our breathing, henki translates to breath. Then there is the itse. The main soul. It enters the body during the first few days of life and survives the body beyond death.

Lastly, we have the luonto. That's the guardian spirit, the protector of the individual. It's also associated with nature and animals. Was John my luonto? He seemed to fit the bill. If so, I wondered how many souls he was responsible for? Must keep him run off his paws, I'd best not pester him about it. I'd try not to anyway. No promises.

Well, that was all very interesting, passed an hour or so. From the noises emanating from John's direction, he was still busy walloping those pesky zombies. I hoped that's what he was up to anyway, a lot of groaning and moaning emanating from his console.

John paused his game. "A guardian of sorts, Whiskers." He raised a finger in the air. "Up to a point. In time, I think, I hope that I'll consider you as more of a colleague." Any opportunity to respond was curtailed by the finger which stayed erect in the space between us for several seconds before pouncing towards his D-pad as he resumed his zombie bashing.

A colleague, hey? Well, that's interesting, not sure how I feel about that, sounds like a lot of work.

We'd be landing in Helsinki soon by the looks of it. Flight attendants were in motion, checking overhead storage, bings and bongs from the panels above our heads. Fasten your seat belts, put out that cigarette that you weren't allowed to smoke in the first place. Thanks for that, I thought, as my craving returned.

The patchwork of green and brown squares below gave way to a more urban, top-down view and as we dropped down from the heavens, the city took shape: lots of pleasant lakes and rivers contrasted with the varied pastel hues of the roofs. Then bump, rumble, rumble, judder, frump and we were down. The bings and bongs returned and a collective sigh of relief was heard as in unison we unleashed our bellies from the restraints.

I'd asked John if we could just relax, have a couple of nights in Helsinki before we headed east to Imatra. I had watched a few walking tours, travel vlogs on YouTube and was keen to make the most of this opportunity.

I'm not a big fan of cities. Noisy, dirty, too busy, just illogically set out in my eyes. Some see them as the pinnacle of our civilisation. Not me. A small town, the countryside, an isolated cove. That's more my cup of tea.

Helsinki was added to a small list of exceptions, the type that would fit on a raffle ticket. John wasn't arguing.

He seemed quite taken by the place, if not the plethora of mean-spirited creatures that claimed residency in the mountains and stretches of water that covered the majority of this fascinating country.

"I really can't stomach… if I had one… any more nasty weirdo creatures for the time being, Whiskers. I have it on good authority. Don't ask! That there is nothing to be learnt from the 'mythological' community on this leg of our journey. The nasties will just try and send us up the wrong path or play with us. They're so bored and pathetic really. They find it more and more difficult to torment the locals these days."

"Why is that?" I asked.

"Less superstitious, stuck to their smartphones, a belief that everything is fake news? A multitude of reasons. Our presence will have ears standing to attention, eyes widened. We're something that's been lacking in their twisted existence."

"What's that?" Why? What? I sounded like a two-year-old, didn't want to interrupt his flow though.

"A challenge, Whiskers. Believers. Belief is a strong emotion and has the power to embolden and make real, give something form. So, we're not going to play that game. I do however want to pay a visit to an old, let's say, acquaintance. You can come with, please? She's quite interesting, in a self-absorbed way, nice though, you could say she has her head in the clouds."

John chuckled to himself, made that punchline gesture, you know as if hitting a drum followed by a cymbal. I let that one go, I was sure I'd get the joke, in time.

"Need a chaperone, do you?"

"Perhaps," came John's coy reply.

Accordingly, we spent a wonderful couple of days mooching around the city. It was July and the weather was pleasantly warm at this time of year. Our base of operations, or lack thereof was the impressive and luxuriant Kämp hotel, complete with spa and art collection, art space? Well, whatever you call it, most impressive.

We were only there a couple of days, but we crammed plenty in, without running about like lunatics late for an appointment: evening strolls along the 'Esplanadi', stopping here and there to enjoy some musical performance, or people watching for a minute or two, John from a bench, me by his side puffing on a woodbine. Then off for some food, a side-street café or more glamorous rooftop bar.

Given its geography, Finnish cuisine is dominated by fish dishes. Not my bag, but John relished it. No Linford's, sorry, battered sausages on the menu over here. The nearest Finnish equivalent I could find was called a 'Nakki', quite an off-putting name to these English ears, and in size, they certainly don't cut the mustard. They really don't know what they're missing!

On our second evening, John said that he'd chosen a special restaurant… festooned with fish of all shapes and colours.

"I can almost smell it from here, Whiskers, can't you?" he grinned and I groaned.

When we rocked up at the joint, I was pleasantly

surprised. He's a good egg is our John. It was a Greek, 'Taverna Zorbas'.

John knows I love Greek food and appreciated that I'd gone with the flow up to this point. There was still a variety of fish on the menu, so we were both happy.

"This one is on you, mind!" said John, a mischievous twinkle brightening his eyes.

"Fine by me, Mr Willis," I replied, beaming.

By day we enjoyed a leisurely breakfast back at the hotel, had a wander around, checked out the museum and the Temppeliaukio church. John went off for a vintage tram ride, no comment, whilst I had a beer and guarded his.

All very chilled. Cat naps in the afternoon, an activity we both seem to enjoy, separately you understand.

So, to sum up: great weather, reserved but welcoming people, interesting, but delicious food, plenty of long drinks, Lonkero to the locals. Cheers or 'kippis', say I. And with that, on with the tale.

Thursday morning, time to head to Imatra. To work and play. En route an appointment with this mystery woman, albeit now with a name: Ilmatar.

So Ilmatar then Imatra, sorry, couldn't resist.

How did you get to Imatra, I hear you ask. I won't dignify that with an answer. You know very well!

I'd noticed that John had changed form once more. No longer the weather-beaten, 'slightly' rotund sports photographer. He now cut a dashing figure. He resembled some sort of 1960s Greek film star. Jet black hair, olive skin. Chiselled features, white open necked shirt, tight black trousers. He must have gained inspiration from one of the waiters in the taverna. I'd checked to see if he had a pair of bread sticks in his back pocket, that's an Italian thing though, I pondered. Anyway, use your imagination, fill in the gaps, picture him to suit your own personal preferences, ladies and gentlemen.

I did think John was above all that lark. I know he is. Maybe this Ilmatar person isn't? I decided against winding him up, for now.

We hopped off the train at Joutseno and set off in search of the lady in question. John took the lead as I dutifully followed. The meeting place, Saimaa, the biggest of Finland's many, thousands of lakes.

It was deathly quiet when we reached a secluded area on the shores of the lake. John stepped forward and at once the surface rippled, parted and from within emerged beauty, wisdom. I was taken aback, like breathing in sharp cold air on a winter's morning. Ilmatar settled on the water's surface, a shimmering vision of... well, like I said, beauty.

She smiled towards John, nodding. I presumed she found his current form agreeable. The eyes, I couldn't define them by colour alone, they appeared to sparkle with the glint of a thousand stars, like miniature globe encased universes. Those enchanting orbs focused in on yours truly, a veritable scruff bag compared to old handsome features over there.

She looked me up and down, from head to toe, a quizzical smile forming, raised eyebrow. Her focus returned to John. I presumed they were communicating in some way or another. I'd been distracted by movement and song. An eagle soaring above the trees, back and forth riding on the currents of the air. If this display was mesmerising, then the song was both confusing and hypnotising. It seemed to emanate from all around, from within the woods but at the same time, inside of me, in my mind. I say song, but it was hard to make out any words, like a murmur, the combined sound of the forces of nature and the animal inhabitants of the surrounding area.

I don't know how long I stood in this dream-like state, but when I did snap out of it, Ilmatar was gone and it was John staring at me, an amused look on his handsome face. The lake was serene, the woods quiet. You know that silence before the rain comes. It didn't, by the way, thankfully.

We set off back to complete our journey to Imatra. John seemed very cock a hoop. I wouldn't have been surprised if he'd broken into a whistle, clicked his heels and such. I broke the ice.

"Bit full of herself, isn't she?" Instantly feeling guilty.

"Well, you've been praised before. How did it make you feel? Spring in your step, slight swelling of the cranium?"

"Well…" I mumbled as way of a reply.

"Imagine being praised throughout your entire existence, for countless millennia. It's like ego-washing, bound to affect even the most modest of creatures."

Duly admonished, I apologised. Directed towards John, meant for Ilmatar.

John had put a friendly arm around my shoulder. What was he on?

"I understand, Whiskers. These are celestial beings. A bit overwhelming to a mere mortal, I'm sure. Let me tell you what she had to say, well, some of it. I'll cut out the personal stuff, don't want you blushing now, do I? She's been up in the stars doing goddess-type things, but her son Väinämöinen sent word to her, drew her back to the lakes. He sensed I was back in town, and was also concerned with the current situation. He likes harmony, nature and, to be honest, I think he was wary of the pair of us stirring things up amongst the more unsavoury characters that inhabit parts of this land. I reassured Ilmatar, told her that I foresee no problems arising, that we'd actually made sure to avoid any nasties. We are on a working holiday, pure and simple."

"So how long was I in that stupor, in a daze? What was with the eagle, the forest song?"

"Well, you were reading all about it on the flight; you should concentrate more, instead of peering over my shoulder."

I took that as an instruction to work it out for myself. As far as the time that passed, it was a minute or two in what counts for time down here, in this reality.

"For me, where I was, it was a pleasant, very productive hour or three." John winked.

He was just winding me up. I wasn't going to dignify him with any reaction. Oh yes, and my mind was locked tight, no leaks there either. Mind you, locking one's thoughts down, was a bit of a reaction in and of itself, wasn't it? Whatever! And since when have I ever said 'one's thoughts'? I think my head was spangled. The sooner I got into that race paddock the better.

It was my first experience of Imatra, although I'd watched it from afar. What a stunning location for a race weekend. The circuit is surrounded by wooded areas and the main straight sits alongside the Vuoksi river. Lakes, stretches of water as I now know, aren't uncommon round this neck of the woods. However, this made the place no less spectacular.

Uniquely, as far as I know, this must be the only race track that features a train track that crosses over the circuit. Wisely, the trains don't run during the event.

Thankfully, we arrived in time for the evening riders' parade and musical entertainment in Inkerinauko city centre. I imagine people are predominantly attracted to the actual high-speed thrills of the racing. As am I, but I love, in equal measure, all the other stuff: the interaction with the riders and teams, the noises, smells that make up the atmosphere in the paddock.

I was really pleased with my report. Happiness is a key ingredient when writing. John was also happy with his images. I think he enjoyed the contrast between machinery and nature.

This relaxed approach to our work was most likely aided by the halt to racing on Sunday. Unusually it slashed it down. From what I've read and viewed it's tended towards blazing hot in recent years. It didn't dampen our spirits though and this was reflected in our results.

The racing highlight for me? The GP250 class. Love those. John? You'll have to ask him. I think he has a secret affection for the 'slideys'. That's the sidecars to you and me.

There was no messing about once the event was over. A short walk, portal and back in sunny Scarborough. John had located another portal close by. I must find out how he does that. I reckon he uses them, the fixed ones when it's convenient or the conventional journey involved to get home doesn't appeal to him. The personal portal, I think he uses that sparingly, maybe those are traceable, less secure. They seem to be the favoured option when he feels that one or both of us are vulnerable, danger imminent. I'll be able to figure that one out myself, over time. Hopefully danger doesn't dictate the method of travel too regularly!

Näkemiin Suomi!

Goodbye Finland!

Next stop, Prague.

PRAGUE

I'd said next stop Prague, but that was the upcoming alighting destination on this adventure of ours. In the meantime, it was back to life, back to reality.

We'd returned from Finland, filed our report, uploaded the images and waited for our next assignment. The fourth round of the IRRC would be held in Chimay, Belgium at the back end of July. Steve Rial rang me up asking if we could cover the Cock o' the North at Oliver's Mount. Steve and son Stevie fancied a change of scenery and wanted to cover the Belgian round.

No problem. I needed a break from trains. I'd need a rubber ring to sit on at this rate, better still, padded, inflatable trousers.

We settled back into our Scarborough routine, John doing whatever he did, as far as I knew back at Mum's, reverting to his form of choice, the feline variety. Me? A bit of research, of the road racing variety.

To coin a phrase, we were match fit, in terms of reporting and togging, investigating alien skullduggery and the like. Nevertheless, it was time to recharge my batteries, at least. I reckoned John was like that Duracell Bunny! Time to do the normal things of life, dial down the paranormal.

It was a period of calm. However, as the end of July approached, I'd begun pacing, both physically and mentally. I always do that when I'm ready to get a move on. Invariably I'm way too early for social engagements, appointments and the like. When I'm ready, I have to move, don't care where, as long as I'm in motion.

Finally! The day had arrived. Time to get a groove on. Our next overseas reporting assignment would be in the Czech Republic, Hořice to be exact.

I'd told John that it was about time we used the portal, direct to our destination, no mucking about. A compromise was settled on, portal to Vienna, train to Prague. It was still four hours of callus-inducing lower cheeks punishment, but it was agreeable.

Vienna is an interesting place: lots of nice architecture to admire and the train journey was supposed to have a picturesque backdrop.

I picked John up on Tuesday morning. A bit previous, but remember 'pacing'. John remarked that he preferred the red van. That had met its maker, rotten to the core, a new to me black Peugeot Expert taking its place.

"Bit sinister looking, Men in Black!" Mum had agreed.

"Whatever! Jump in." John was still in cat form.

"Why?" said I.

"I find it more comfortable, portal wise."

"Yeah? So, it's me the nominated Sherpa then? Don't you worry, I'll get your bag."

A five-minute drive, despite the eleven speed humps that separated my Mum's house in the suburbs from Lisa's house in town. A fortuitous parking spot right outside the house was a good start. I spend far too much time worrying about such matters. Lisa and Winnie were out at her Mum and Dad's in Cloughton, so I placed the van keys on the computer table in the dining room.

Had a scan round, as you do and satisfied that all was in its place, we set off to the portal, located a couple of hundred yards from Murchison Street, in Dean Road cemetery. John kept a few cat steps behind, like one of those moggies who insist on following you up the street. They only do it to wind you up, you know.

A quick glance here and there. All clear. John, ever the professional, made some sort of hazy thing in the tunnel to further camouflage our disappearance. Swirly time. I was getting used to it now.

We re-appeared in the Zentralfriedhof cemetery in Vienna. Why always with those? A bit clichéd. Anyway, John masked our arrival again and we strode out from the shadows and headed off into the city centre. A ten-minute walk, tram, another leg-stretch, tram, walk and we were there: Vienna Central station.

It was still early. People were scurrying to and fro, a zig zag of Austrians, obviously delighted, enthusiastic to start the work day.

We had about forty minutes to waste before the ten past nine 'railjet' to Prague.

Not entirely wasted though, there were plenty of interesting places just a stone's throw from the train station, unfortunately some yet to open, not enough time to spare. Maybe some other time, but for now we settled on The Hofsburg, an impressive building, for centuries the centre of the Habsburg empire, now home to several museums. No time for those, not open until nine anyway.

We satisfied ourselves with a coffee. John now in

human form, we sat on a bench and admired the architectural splendour. Coffee maybe, but I was aware that such an ostentatious display of wealth and power wasn't everybody's cup of tea. Well, we liked it anyway. Wouldn't want to live there though: too roomy for me, rather a crofter's cottage for this wannabe hermit.

Anyway, I digress. Train to catch, buttock pain incoming… steady now!

We arrived. Prague Hlavni Nadrazi. That's main station to the English speakers amongst us. This was the end of the line for John, at least until Hořice at the weekend. Arrangements made, he was off, "To see a man about a dog." He reasoned I'd be more of a carrot, seemingly vulnerable to our adversaries if they thought I was alone. I would be alone! We'd be connected, he had assured me. Anyway, he'd soon be back by my side, that is, if there was a train to Hořice. If not, he would see me trackside, at the circuit.

And with that he was off, immediately running across the strasse directly into the path of a tram, forgetting he was in human form, as opposed to being a cat.

I called out to him and he ran back, narrowly avoiding another.

"What?" he said.

Farewell temporarily halted, we briefly discussed his mortality, or lack thereof. Typical me, typical Whiskers. I needed to know, now it was in my head. I must say John could be very patient with this mere mortal at times.

He talked rapidly, breathlessly for effect. Probably, no definitely, to indicate that this was a conversation for another time, place. Something along these lines: although alive, more created than born and besides he occupied several points in time and space at once. Could phase in and out of this or that reality. I convinced myself that I understood, nodded. No further discussion required and he was off again. I did a 180 and headed off, destination undecided. I guarantee he'd have chosen another death-defying route, just to wind me up. I sensed his frustration via our mental connection, thwarted by that pesky human again. Hee hee! One nil to Whiskers.

So, here was I, Billy no mates, Larry lonesome, alone. Suited me, I'm pretty self-reliant. I reached out to Bohemia Interactive, the games developer based in Prague. It was a long shot, but I fancied a tour round their offices. I'd seen in the past that they'd obliged others, then taken them for a pint or two.

Given their games portfolio, did I mention I'm a huge fan of DayZ? It crossed my mind whether there were any evil geniuses at work or play at the house of Bohemia… Interactive. No such luck in that regard, but they didn't disappoint and I had a meeting scheduled with Scott Bowen, the DayZ brand manager, no less. I was in gamer heaven. Someone once wrote: a culture without games was no culture at all. Not sure if that's a real quote. Well, it should be. I'll claim it then. Whoever it was, if anyone, I doubt he or she had poking the undead in the eye with a pointy stick in mind when they said it. But the 'point' ha ha… still stands…. unlike the zombie twitching at my feet. Anyway, Scott and I were later joined by Pavel Křižka and Tomáš Přibyl for a few cold ones and a good old chinwag. The weather was glorious and the beer and company were both top notch.

A good start to my Prague trip, we bid our farewells and I wandered away from the Císařská louki and headed off in search of an Irish bar, McCarthy's. Something to eat and I set about booking into one of the hotels the lads had recommended. Job done, a Guinness and off to the Metropolitan for an early night.

Up and at 'em early Wednesday. A wander around the city visiting the Old Town Hall to see the astronomical clock, followed by the Museum of Alchemy – Speculum Alchemiae. Fascinating places, both, in entirely different ways. By lunchtime I'd overloaded on culture, too much of a good thing and such. I sat myself down on a bench in Letná park. I seem to like benches, don't I? Anyway, decisions, decisions, the afternoon and evening were ahead of me.

As I'd said before, John had disappeared – figuratively this time. So here was I: 'old, free and spoken for.' So, what to do? Prague, time on my hands, ha! Sunny day. Answer? Cold beer and people watching. I weighed anchor at the Hotel U Prince, one of a myriad of hotels with pleasant bars and outside seating areas, perfect for whiling away the hours, watching the world go by. I'd noticed they had another bar located in the basement. It was called the Black Angel's Bar. I thought I'd give that a miss. No thank you very much, not without my sidekick. I was getting more confident each and every day, but nooooo! I was happy enough having a pint on my own, solo, 'on me tod.' I may be self-contained, but that didn't mitigate the age-old problem. What to do when you need to visit the little boy's room? I resorted to my tried and tested tactics, namely, get talking to someone, once the rapport is built, ask them to keep an eye on your gear… 'cough'… beer. The victims in question, a 'mature' couple from the UK. The bloke, a Geordie, 'Kev', his head adorned with an impressive mane of bright white hair; a jovial, cheeky specimen. No malice to this one. The lady, Sandra, quiet, softly spoken, hard to read, the Sophia Loren-esque voluminous sunglasses adding to the sense of mystique. A relaxed, entertaining and semi-drunken afternoon ensued. That merry, smiley, Sid James laughing-type of inebriation. Eventually, as all good things do, it came the time to part ways, farewells and promises to look each other up, when back in 'Blighty'. Sandra raised her sunglasses, eyes, twin penetrating orbs of sapphire. A wink. A postcard folded in two, placed surreptitiously on my table. The content? A name, a location. Mr Pojer, Berlin. The game was afoot! One more pint of 'Urquell', though: rude not to, 'when in Prague'.

Thursday morning, after a good night's sleep. Odd for me, head hitting the pillow and 'sparko'. I suppose the sun and beer must have helped. Okay, okay, it most definitely did. No harm, no foul.

Breakfast, continental, and off to meet John. He'd messaged me a time and place, no handheld devices required for our communication. You know that by now.

The train station… again! A sense of someone watching, infiltrating my mind space. Probing soon halted. By distraction more than mental fortitude. John leant against a humongous black limousine, a Maybach, no less. He was grinning ear to ear like a Cheshire cat. One all! He's a one is our John!

Hořice. What a track! What a weekend from start to finish! Arriving in style thanks to John, and from the moment we stepped out of our five-star apartment on wheels until we portalled back to Scarborough, we had a blast.

NO, REALLY, WHAT'S THE CRAIC?

So much had happened over the last few months since my mini-briefing from John. We'd been here, there and everywhere, reporting on different races, visiting several cities, stared blankly out of train windows for hours on end.

I'd encountered several parties who were interested in our adventure, some hostile, some friendly and others… well, I'm not sure what side of the fence they were on.

I needed a bit more info from John. What the state of play was, what went before the here and now that led to the current situation. On a personal level, I was curious as to how we were progressing and where that would inevitably lead us. I've come to realise, in the last couple of minutes, that I have a fair idea of my place in, and the majority of elements of this puzzle. It feels a bit like the famous Eric Morcambe quote when explaining his piano playing to pianist Andre Previn: 'I'm playing all the right notes, but not necessarily in the right order'. I'll get there, I have no doubt.

Why now? Why was I about to embark on one of my infamous, annoying Whiskers-John Willis Q&A sessions? Oh, and another puzzle to solve or resolve: one word, well, two. Albert Ross. I'll get into that later, first things first: question time.

I messaged John, no, not by smart phone, you know

the score, a mind message if you like. Obviously, he knew what was on my mind, most likely before I did. Was nothing sacred? Mum was out, at her art group down at Scalby Library. She'd be gone for an hour or two.

'Won't take that long,' John interjected… mind message!

We settled in the lounge, John back in cat form, his go to. I think John would quite happily spend the rest of his days, eternity occupying his favoured feline representation. The only reason he reverts to a human likeness is in order not to attract unwanted attention when he's amongst the likes of you and I. Let's be serious for a moment, when he was passing himself off as a sports photographer, he'd have looked a bit daft, a moggie with a camera slung around his neck, wouldn't he? Cameras may have shrunk over recent times, but no, bona fide sports photographers still use lenses the size of traffic cones.

"So, John, what's the craic?"

"The craic?"

He seemed distracted. What was he worried about? Was everything going to plan? I mused. Then I spotted it. A multi coloured ball of yarn on the floor adjacent to John. I glanced surreptitiously, well, a pretence thereof, arched a brow.

"Don't even," John whispered. He knows I detest whispering.

Must have some residual cattiness I pondered as I saw one set of claws retract into an ebony-furred paw.

Whispering? It annoys me. You can still hear what people are saying, just in an irritating tone. Either go to another room to plot or just talk out loud and be done with it! Who's distracted now? Me! I snapped out of it and regained my focus.

"The craic, the gen, the 411. In short, what's going on?"

"Ahhh! Can you narrow that down? Try and organise your thoughts, your words, Whiskers."

I frowned and transitioned to a grin.

"Well, we've been to many places recently, met some interesting people, things? Ruby, Kev and Sandra, Bunny. Then we have this Mr Pojer. Do we meet with him? There is also the question of this fellow who seems to be shadowing me. Do we introduce ourselves? What's all this about Bulgaria?"

"So many questions, hardly organised though."

"There's more…"

"I thought there might be…"

John's tail wafted from side to side, not a good sign, in any form of feline.

Okay, organisation mode activated.

I held up a single digit. "How are we progressing and where do you think said progress is leading us, location wise?" Two fingers raised, politely. "Why are these particular aliens trying to thwart us, if they indeed are, and what is their over-arching strategy, their motive?" Three fingers. "Can you give me the low-down on the players, the movers and shakers in this drama of ours?"

John cleared his throat, no, not an errant furball.

I saw my chance and quickly added another question, not enough time for four fingers. "Are the demony, evil-type creatures assisting these xenophobic aliens, or keeping a watching brief, bowl of popcorn to hand or claw?"

"Finished?"

I strained my brain. "Yes, thank you, John."

John nodded, raised a paw as if to hold up one finger, thought better of it and began to talk, to enlighten me… I hoped.

"Progress, yes, Whiskers, we are making satisfactory progress. You've come on in leaps and bounds. Don't blush, you know you have. These many, many questions are a reflection of this advancement, this justified confidence. I have no worries on that score. Don't let it go to your head though. Keep working on your mental strength and such. There is no handbook, so learn by doing, let it come to you naturally. As far as this adventure, this quest, whatever you want to call it, yes, I'm very pleased. These trips to Europe have drawn out friend and foe alike, which is what I was hoping for from the off. I now know where the end game will take place and have a good idea who and what our nemesis is. Yes, nemesis, one entity, a lone creature. However, not working alone. Let's call him a 'he' for now. He is obviously pulling the strings, silky ones."

John chuckled to himself. I let it go, didn't want him to lose… his thread… I returned the chuckle, which went unnoticed.

"The reason for all of this subterfuge? The motives.

I'll give you the party line, Whiskers, because, well, it's largely accurate. This comes from my masters, for want of a better word. Simply put, these xenophobic aliens, albeit a particularly aggressive element of their race, for not all are fanatics, wish to wipe humanity off the face of this earth. They certainly don't want to see your race reach for the stars. There's no refinement, no subtlety. It's as basic as that. Kill all humans! One way or the other."

John paused. I took the momentary silence as an invitation to talk.

I nodded, squished and contorted my lips, like a novice wine taster. "Instead of encouraging humans to destroy themselves, exploiting resources, tearing down nature, becoming embroiled in border disputes, hot wars, why don't these xenophobic aliens flip it on its head and create a utopia, so the human race just gently dies out and fades away, stops procreating, becomes over reliant on machines, like so many other races? ...I imagine."

"They're xenophobic, warlike, a warrior race, they aren't into nuance. They want to destroy their quarry violently, have their prey know the taste of defeat and see the face of their conquerors as they draw a last breath. Unfortunately, for them, they don't have the numbers to carry out a conventional act of genocide on the human race. They're hamstrung by the very thing that makes them so aggressive. They effectively almost wiped themselves out as a species. Being dyed-in-the-wool xenophobes, they didn't like the cut of their own jib: clan wars, caste systems, regional conflicts. They weren't all crazed blood-thirsty loons however. Parts of their society broke away, transcended, if you will. The vast majority of the aforementioned transcended are isolationists, no longer interested in the machinations of their barbaric brothers and sisters. They keep out of universal affairs for the most part. However, a small number of enlightened beings try their best to guide their brethren away from such idiocy and in turn try to protect those threatened species. The xenophobes are forced down the path of asymmetrical warfare, much to their chagrin, so, if it's a choice between boring a civilisation to death, or getting them to bore holes in each other, they choose the latter."

I nodded, again. Seemed to be doing a lot of that. Couldn't be good for the old Gregory Peck... that's neck by the way.

John took my head-bobbing as a sign of understanding on my part. He wasn't wholly far from the truth.

"Back to your three 'finger-questions'... in no particular order. The demony creatures, as you referred to them, well, we discussed that the last time we had one of these over-questiony conversations. I'll elaborate though. The demonic Satan-led forces are torn, in a quandary. Yes, their remit is to ultimately destroy mankind, but the feeling is that they've become accustomed to the status quo. I think they have long realised that their ultimate goal is unachievable, not that they would care to admit to it. However, they do take the view that if they meddle here, torment there, the human species will, over time, become the masters of their own demise. Be mindful, in this game, 'over time' can be thought of in the thousands, maybe tens of thousands, of years. To beings who could be classed as immortal, the time-frame is irrelevant. They don't exist in the same time and space as you understand it. They walk the line between linear and non-linear time. Suffice to say, they don't clock-watch, buy a new calendar every year. I think they deem this alien project as doomed to failure. Unfortunately for them, they can do no other. It would be an admittance of failure on their part, if these alien interlopers waltz in and achieve in a jiffy what they've failed to accomplish in thousands of years. Don't get me wrong. They're enjoying the show. They won't go as far as joining forces on the battlefield, not that the xenophobes would welcome that idea either. They will however, interfere here and there, try to control the pieces on the board. A proxy war of sorts. Maybe they've left a skeleton – ha! – staff behind and all gone on holiday to the Costa del Hades. We need to be mindful that they are most certainly a major player in the neighbourhood, without allowing ourselves to become distracted from our main focus, the xenophobes. This hodgepodge of characters that we've met on our travels, they aren't anything to worry about. There will be other interested parties willing to help you during your quest."

"Calm down, Gandalf."

John rolled his eyes. "Journey then. Some benevolent, some with more treacherous motives. We'll deal with all of that when encountered."

"Seems a bit blasé?" I suggested.

"I agree, I am, completely. It's not worth the effort,

pontificating on the things we have no control over. I like to use that energy to visualise the big picture, really exercise those little grey cells. All we can do is deal with any interlocuters on a case-by-case basis, Whiskers. 'It'll be reet' as Guy says." John referring to the TT racer turned TV presenter and housewife's favourite, Guy Martin.

It always makes me laugh when John references something from what I think of as my world, I suppose I'm late to the party. This is his planet, every bit as much as mine.

"You should be in your element, Whiskers. You spend far too much time lying in bed worrying about all the things that can go wrong. Pandemics, wars, whether or not your van will break down, what if you choke on this 'Cheesy Wotsit'. Well, it's good to be prepared, hope for the best and all that, but not to the detriment of your mental well-being. Besides, all these forebodings, imaginary or not, well, they've come home to roost. You should be happy, Whiskers!"

He flicked me with his tail. I began to nod, turned it into a head dip and broad smile.

"As for your non-raised finger question."

He noted my confused, stunned mullet look.

"Bulgaria!"

"Ah yes, Ruby mentioned Bulgaria, didn't he?"

"He did indeed. I've been sending out feelers, using my own contacts. I can say with confidence that Ruby was most definitely on the money. Our nemesis is most assuredly ensconced in Bulgaria, Tsarichina to be exact."

"But what is it, who is it, why…?"

John Willis held up a paw.

"Patience, Whiskers. Relax! Besides, I don't have all the answers, yet, and Rome wasn't built in a day. Strange saying. Who actually thought it was? The important things, their buildings, their art, philosophy remain to this day. Still relevant, physical. Important in the grand scheme of things? That's subjective. Built good roads, though."

Anticipating my sigh of frustration, John snapped out of his imperial musings.

He cleared his throat. "Anyway, I digress. This thing, this alien, whatever, has switched gears. Decided that this is the time to go on the offensive. Whereas in the past it took on the role of puppet master, sending out underlings to whisper in the ears of politicians, civil servants, activists etc. Wheedling his way into the inner circles in order to stir things up, sow discord. Like Rasputin or Lucius Detritus, the Roman agent in that cartoon movie: Asterix and Obelisk Vs Caesar. He's existed on the periphery, concentrating his efforts on the whisperers, apologists, propagandists or in modern day parlance… influencers." He groaned. "Well, for reasons unknown, he's gone all in. Maybe it's something to do with our appearance on the field, perhaps it's all a bluff. Alternatively, it could be you, me or both of us that are the target. It makes no difference. We have our task and it doesn't matter who the opposition is and what ulterior motives drive them to do what they do. We'll smash them either way!"

"Yes!" I exclaimed.

"I know what you think about this whole road racing gig, Whiskers. A charade? No, self-indulgence? Well, partly."

•

John here again, just to be clear. Whiskers thought the RRN gig was pure indulgence on my part. Not that he was complaining.

However, it had proved extremely useful, to me. I felt like the pied piper, drawing out all these interested parties from within the shadows. Not all rats. Friends and foes alike. Made life a lot easier. I didn't know all, too many variables involved to predict the future with any degree of certainty. I wasn't the only talent in this cast of players.

•

"Well, I did wonder," I replied, scratching my scalp to indicate a slight level of confusion.

"Our adversaries' web encompasses the entirety of Eastern Europe," John Willis said. "Why there? Superstitious people keep away from notorious areas, authorities want to keep it quiet. Unlike the West where it's based on fear, this cover up is fuelled by pride. What we need is the proverbial Ken Dodd tickling stick, a blooming big one at that."

"Tickling stick?"

"Clean up this mess, remove the web."

"It sounds like the Joseph Conrad novel, Heart of Darkness."

"Yes, you're right, Whiskers, but there are a few twists and turns left on this journey up the river. The next move, your next move… before you ask: You need to deal with someone…" another waft of his tail. "…who's been tailing you. You'll be doing the talking, surprise, surprise."

"And your role, John?"

"Well, the muscle obviously."

Parles concluded, a bit more in the know than beforehand, I decided to leave John in peace for a day or two, go and do a bit of solo sleuthing. That could wait until tomorrow though. I had a different mission on my mind, a couple of thimbles in the Traf, to digest all I'd been told, before I went blundering about doing agenty things.

ME AND MY SHADOW

Albert Ross! I mean, where do these idiots get these cover names? Bird brains! Ha!

Anyway, I'm getting ahead of myself. You remember I'd informed Whiskers that he was being tailed? Are you sitting comfortably? Good! Over to Whiskers to explain how he met 'Albatross'.

•

As we'd concluded our recent pow-wow, John had mentioned that some person unknown, to me, had been following me about.

Now that I come to mention it, I think that deep down I was aware of his presence, tingling spidey-senses and all that. I was just too preoccupied with our travels, with the Bunny interaction still at the forefront too.

I'd been coming out of Nige's corner shop on Columbus Ravine, a stone's throw from our house. My usual Wednesday routine: some gammon trim for me and Winnie, mostly for her. That distinctive odour. Smelt that before. Cigar. I'm no expert, sommelier of brown smelly tubes. Smelt expensive though. Being a smoker, I just filter out the aroma of my own ash-sodden attire. Smoke emanating from a car window, red. Where have I smelt that before? Ah! Yes, in Beverley, that was it. Different car, same smell though. More than a coincidence.

I made a mental note: no further action at this juncture. I'd see how things panned out. I had let John know and he advised me to contact him the next time I spotted this nosey parker.

We'd agreed that I should, if I encountered his presence in the coming days, lead him to somewhere secluded… for a little chat. Sounded a bit ominous, but I think he did really mean a word in the ear. No 'Goodfellows' shenanigans on the menu.

I'd taken a drive up to Oliver's Mount. Perfect. Open areas combined with the odd secluded corner and not overly busy at this time of year. John would make his own way up, most probably utilising a portal. We'd informed Trevor, out of common courtesy. I'd parked up close to the farmhouse where my pal 'Trigger' lived and strolled across the field towards the bridge that crosses the esses section of the track.

I'd thought about taking Winnie for added authenticity, but had decided against it. I didn't know what we were dealing with and wanted to control the 'sting', not put Winnie in harm's way, and have her being stung.

I smelt the cigar smoke at the same time as I spotted the little red car, parked on the service road about two hundred metres from where I was stood. No messing around, not even checking whether my sidekick had arrived yet. I strolled purposefully over and tapped on the driver's window, smoke emanating, billowing from within as it was partially wound down.

"You've been following me. Care to explain yourself, put a name to your face?"

This pro-active approach worked wonders. The fellow, clearly startled, wound his window down. Never even complained when I swiftly removed the key from the ignition. At this point, John appeared from behind a tree and strolled over, a military bearing, hands clasped behind his back. He came to a halt about a yard behind me, visible to the accused over my right shoulder. Albert Ross AKA Smokey Joe, introduced himself, as best you can, through a car window, hand outstretched.

"Albert Ross, I'm Albert... um... Ross."

Using his name as a safety blanket, to reassure himself. Trouble was, he didn't believe it any more than I did. Admittedly, he was startled. As I said, I'd marched up to his car and challenged him, sick of the intrigue. Taking all of that into account, he was still utterly unconvincing. People don't usually introduce themselves like that, not these days anyway. It was laughable: trilby, regimental tie, long beige raincoat. Burberry? Been watching too many 1960s cold war dramas. It couldn't be that his masters were only seeing those now, that thing about TV and radio signals taking so long to travel the stars, because according to John, these beings have been on the planet far longer than you and I.

Conclusion: banana brains... a bunch of. His reply to my challenge?

"I've been tasked to keep an eye on you, and your chum... me? Ex-military."

He flicked his tie as if to prove the point.

"Retired now. Not sure of the whys and wherefores, old boy."

I'd 'old boy' him in a minute!

"Your controller?"

"Spook, Whitehall chappy, went to a good school, Rugger type. Ours is not to reason why. Bit bored at the time, at a loose end since leaving the regiment. Getting under the feet of 'she who must be obeyed'. Felt wanted, needed again. Useful. King and Country and all that."

I almost 'pitied the fool', almost. So that was the defence, which I tended to believe, now for the prosecution. Step forward, Mr Willis, the floor is yours, I'd mind messaged John. No longer a novelty to me, using the method instinctively. He stepped forward as I'd taken two back.

'Perfect timing, Whiskers,' he thought. 'We really are gelling. Willis of the Bailey incoming.'

No introduction. Straight into it. Don't give him time to think.

"Well, I have to inform you, Mr 'Albert Ross'..." John's best Scotland Yard impression was in full effect. "...that you are in fact, working for the opposition, not King and Country as you most patriotically put it. I mean, even those dullards in Whitehall wouldn't have used such a ridiculous cover name for their new, most prized asset." Albert's face a picture of confusion, John Willis enlightened him. "It's preposterous! Albatross... Albert Ross."

Albert reddened, moustaches twisting, almost tying themselves into a knot. No. He didn't have two moustaches! It's what they call it: saw it on an episode of Poirot, I think. Doubting myself now. One moment, yes! I was correct, little grey cells are obviously in tip-top shape.

John continued. "From my perspective, Albert, you have a couple of choices. Stand down before Mr Whiskers over there is let off his leash."

I thought John was meant to be the muscle in this game of good cop, bad cop, but I kept my counsel, not wanting to disturb John's flow. These things are dynamic, I concluded.

"Believe me, you wouldn't want that," John was saying. "Or you can step up and really serve your King, humanity and start helping us, the good guys. Given the crowd you've fallen in with, standing down completely might just be detrimental to your well-being... old boy. You're trapped within this house of cards now anyway and I very much doubt your current masters will invest in your future well-being regardless of whether you carry out their orders, complete your tasks. I think you'll be viewed as expendable on completion of your mission. The long-term prognosis is far from rosy. Cheer up, old chap. You're not to blame. Come on now, let's go and have a chat, the three of us."

From the depths of depression, emerged a glimmer of hope and Albert's spirits seemed to lift, moustaches standing at ease. John debriefed Albert, no point changing names now, too confusing. He assured me that from here on in, our agent, Albert, would come to no harm. I, in turn, reassured Mr Ross, although I stated that there were no guarantees. Got to keep him on his brogue-encased toes.

The apron strings had been cut, well, moved. Now under our charge, Albert set off on his way, by the sound of his gear change... crunch, roar, klunk... he obviously wasn't completely at ease, mollified. Well, I had no control over that. What I, well, more likely John, could try to control was his safety.

As we strolled back to the van, John deciding on a more conventional form of transport on the return journey, we, well, he, came up with an action plan, to hopefully ensure Albert could continue picking up his army pension for a few years yet. The conclusion? Albert was to carry on spying, good name for a film that. We wanted him to resume normal service, with a twist. He'd continue to tail me as ordered by his previous masters, and report back, having run everything past us. It would still have to pass muster, be believable. We agreed that we weren't too concerned if the opposition knew about the vast majority of our movements. It had proven profitable so far, them knowing loosely what we were up to. It was a two-way street and exposed as much about their intentions as ours.

We would strongly advise Albert that he show no signs of familiarity, no surreptitious nods of the head, winks of the eye. Not entirely confident he'd resist the urge, but that was out of our hands. We'd made our beds as they say.

On the point of safety, Albert's, if suspicions were raised, he was found wanting, busted as a double, well, John had the solution to that particular quandary.

John had the perfect team for the job, Lola and Luna,

whom he described as his 'favourite mahogany-skinned assassins. No, they weren't made of or clad in that lovely reddish-brown hardwood! It was just the form, the colour they preferred to take these days. Luna the brains, Lola the muscle, infamous within the circles in which John moves. A legendary pairing and most definitely and historically, fighting for good over evil. Their appearance dark, their motives not. The two 'Ls' could shield 'Albatross' from any physical threat directed at his person. If things got hairy in any other way, they could plonk him down a portal for safe keeping. That's the difference between us and the baddies, John explained, eyes fixed on mine, 'We look after our people.' By the way, you may have raised an eyebrow when I mentioned 'assassins' earlier? John had enquired of me. I responded with a shallow nod. John concurred, agreeing that yes, it was a bit old-testament, but that's because we weren't dealing with fluffy kittens here. More like genocidal maniacs! No stroking required, unless with an obsidian blade!

That was our bird problem dealt with. Whether Albatross would reap any rewards was unknown. We'd sorted things on a wing and a prayer. As long as he caused more good than harm, we'd got him out from under his wife's feet and if he didn't come a cropper, I'd be content.

Ultimately, we would soon have bigger fish to fry and in the short-term we had a new player who wished to introduce himself. The name: Mr Pojer. The place: Berlin. No rest for the non-wicked!

CZECH-POINT CHARLIE

Do you recall Prague, the couple I spent a convivial afternoon with? Well, Sandra had passed me that note. A folded postcard with a name: Mr Pojer and a location. I'd not paid much attention to the latter until later. It said: Berlin.

He'd obviously grown impatient, wanted to get something off his chest. No pretence at trade-craft, cloaks and daggers conspicuous in their absence. Simply a polite letter of invitation requesting a meeting during his upcoming art exhibition. The location: Checkpoint Charlie, where else?

We had the place and, thanks to the signature on the note, we had a first name, Peter.

For the uninitiated, the checkpoint is symbolic of the cold war between east and west. A crossing point interrupting the more substantial structures of the Berlin Wall. Immortalised in many a spy film or book, often portrayed as the location of choice where intelligence agents from opposing sides would meet half way to swap captured spies or political prisoners.

This characterisation is grounded in fact. The most famous prisoner exchange has to be that of the American U2 spy plane pilot, Gary Powers, who was exchanged for Rudolf Abel. And no, I didn't just google that, I'm not completely one-dimensional. Not all about bikes, you know, although I do understand how you reached that conclusion.

We portalled in to Berlin. Apparently, there are many such nodes in this part of Germany. Something related to the cold war. Perhaps evacuation points for higher ups, or other worldly observers? Who knows? We arrived, or is it appeared?, within an underground bunker, vast marble concourse, no depressing grey concrete here. At least on the surface… sub-surface as we were.

We emerged from a seldom-used private subway platform, onto the side… strasse?, by way of a nondescript door, me blinking and rubbing at my eyes, John more restrained. Why do we do that? Maybe we've seen it on the silver screen and it's just expected, 'mole-esque' etiquette.

We had time to kill so John suggested that we look for a cinema. I doubted that this early arrival was by mistake. I didn't believe that his suggestion was impromptu either.

John didn't believe in coincidences or accidents, things occurring seemingly out of the blue. There was always a reason, the result of a series of events. I'd come to agree with him, so I knew full well that he'd planned our itinerary well in advance. He must have really wanted to see a film, I concluded. I fell into step. I could hardly complain, I'm famous for arriving early, much to the chagrin of, well, of myself.

If I've got an appointment or arranged to meet a pal for drinks at seven for example, I'll be pacing around from three. It gets to five, I can stand it no longer and I'm out the door. So, it's standing around, after attempting to walk slowly and failing, or in the case of drinks, that's me, three pints deep before my partner in crime joins me. Always the same, no big deal, you may think, but I hate being out of sync when it comes to beverages. I'm slurring while my friend is only in the moronic, grinning, rosy cheeked stage.

John seemed to know where he was heading, so I sauntered along a couple of paces behind. One eye on him, the other set to observation mode. Not on the lookout for furtive interlopers, just people watching. A bit way out around here, I thought. Yes, I know. I'd only been here five minutes, seen a snapshot of the city. Let's just say there was an eclectic mix of characters in this specific area. A lot of arty types, modern day hippies and a greater than average sprinkling of eccentrics.

Not judging, the bigger the melting pot, the better, more interesting to this nosy parker. However, you'd struggle to convince me of your Earth Mother credentials when decked out in tech, iPhone glued to your lug-hole, smart watch taking count of every bare footed step... why?

One colourfully-clothed chap, beard festooned with that many beads I thought he might topple over, approached me, visibly concerned. And there was me worried about the consequences if he added more or grew his chin wig a bit longer.

He was pointing at my head, ranting in German. I quickly realised that he was pointing at my cap. John obviously had a meticulous grasp of the language and duly filled in the gaps.

He was concerned that the silver logo on the brim was some form of receiver, tracking device embedded. In that moment, I'd wished I'd allowed Lisa to peel it off! A fervent peeler is our Lisa.

Anne, at the market back in Scarborough had also alluded to something along similar lines… 'That's how they get you'. I'll have to keep an eye on her, nah! She's just got the same sense of humour as me. Hasn't she?

Anyway, John said something seemingly comforting to the man and, mollified, he'd wandered off contentedly. Maybe we could have read his mind or sent some type of instruction to his subconscious. We don't abuse that power though, and there was no telling how this gentleman was wired.

We resumed our stroll, passing several art house type cinemas. Knowing John, I doubted he would be interested in all of that. After about fifteen minutes, we rocked up at Cinema X on Potsdamer Street. Don't worry, it wasn't one of those cinemas! Besides it'd need two more Xs to qualify, unless one X denotes the mild form of, well, you get my drift. I'm no expert, honest guv!

The Wild Robot was the film of choice. He likes his animation, does our John. I wasn't going to argue. I didn't fancy much else on the audio-visual menu. There were plenty of screens anyway. If I'd have really wanted to see something in particular, I would have. Despite rumours to the contrary, we weren't joined at the hip. I enjoyed the film, a bit over loud, as they tended to be, although I would have welcomed a bit more volume if it would have drowned out the 'coughing man', the choir leader of the resultant frogs' chorus, bear with me. He had one of those nervous, persistent coughs. I call them snooker coughs. Picture the Crucible, in Sheffield. Two players poking their balls with chalk-tipped potting sticks. A cough barks out from the dimly lit arena. The guilty party? A solitary spectator. Within a couple of minutes, a veritable frogs' chorus fills the entire venue. The commentators attempt to counteract this cacophonous anuran racket. Louder and louder, a battle of wills, cough, cough. 'HE'S MISSED THAT LONG PINK BY A MILE, TICKLED THE BROWN. HE WON'T BE HAPPY, HIS FACE A PICTURE OF CONFUSION.' COUGH! COUGH!

Only John and I resisted this siren call... croak! John filtered it out, seemingly engrossed in his film, oblivious. I stubbornly attempted to ignore it, face reddening as I suppressed my animal rage. A bit of an exaggeration. Controlled seething? You know, when your head slowly descends to a level parallel to your shoulders, coiling like a spring, ready to leap and emit a howling war cry.

As we filed out of the screening room and through the lobby, I messaged John. 'Can you gift me that skill?'

'Nothing supernatural, Whiskers, it's simply patience and concentration.'

'Aah, noted.'

'Do as you would when a clock seemingly ticks too loud. Either that, or join in with the chorus of the frogs.'

We met Peter Pojer at Einstein Kaffee, relatively... close to checkpoint Charlie. Okay, it was right on the doorstep. Peter was unassuming, bespectacled and had a playful personality; he radiated fun and good humour.

He was an artist. All round, a creative spirit. His current form of expression was that of mechanical working installations. Think Heath Robinson, but scaled down in size, not function.

He moved in certain influential circles in Prague: diplomats, art and cultural missions, he had the ear of, and was listened to, by the hierarchy. Approachable, friendly, he provided a useful conduit, connecting the establishment and the people, able to cross the divide between the average Joe and the stuffed shirts of officialdom.

He was usually accompanied by his equally artistic, but socially reserved wife, Mariko. However, he'd explained that she was over at the 'Schinkel Pavillon' fine-tuning his exhibits before the grand opening. He didn't like to expose her to this side of his business for fear of her coming to harm. "Not by you," he nodded apologetically to each of us in turn. "I hope you understand this?"

We waved away his apology with synchronised right hands and accompanying reassuring smiles.

Back to Mr Pojer. He represented various Czech-based parties on an ad hoc basis. A committed humanitarian, he was interested not only in domestic concerns, and as such we were convinced that he was firmly on our team, supportive of our cause. With this stance confirmed, we moved on to the substance. What did he have for us? No point beating around the bush once a bond is established.

Peter had information regarding the Bulgarian authorities. High level discussions had taken place between the Czech and Bulgarian foreign offices or their versions of.

A request had been presented and subsequently agreed to by the Bulgarian representatives. We weren't named, identified in the negotiations, but John and I would be granted full access to a restricted zone located in the western region of Bulgaria.

And with that, he downed his cappuccino and contorted his lips in a display of caffeine satisfaction. Vigorous handshakes all round, smiling out of relief and genuine affection, and he was off.

An envelope was the only evidence that he'd been sitting in our company just seconds prior. He'd politely returned his tiny cup and saucer to the counter top and opened the door in one fluid movement.

The envelope contained some coordinates and a codeword. John remarked that the former was of great use, but we would avoid the need to provide the latter if at all possible.

Also included were a couple of tickets to the exhibition. John had sensed my frustrated unease.

"Don't worry, we'll find our way in before the doors open. We'll take a look-see in the wee hours, Whiskers."

I have an aversion to social gatherings where small talk abounds; people who clearly have no interest in the other party, filling the silence with opaque words, waiting to catch the eye of someone more important, with a higher status level. I can't be doing with pretence, false 'bonhomie'. I also don't like abridged things. I want, crave, the long form. Cricket, books, the whole nine yards please. I don't like films based on books. Small talk, no thanks. I want to know it all, the full story, the whole caboodle. Genuine conversations and people please, otherwise I have better things to do, like counting clouds on an overcast day. Exactly, absolutely anything other.

"You still feel up to a quick circuit round the Mauer?"

"Oh, most definitely. Cheers, John!"

The Mauer is the Checkpoint Charlie Museum. Before you start, this isn't the same as the previously explained exhibition anxiety. We wouldn't have to engage with anyone. I doubted there would be any waiting on staff with large silver salvers and inexplicably tiny culinary offerings: stupid miniature sandwiches and vol-au-vents that would have a sparrow reaching for the biscuit barrel. I didn't reckon the museum would be a catered affair. I was a bit peckish, mind. Where's a digestive when you need it?!

I thoroughly enjoyed our Mauer experience, as I do the majority of museums I've visited over the years. Reluctant at first, at the thought of leaving the house, to be honest, glad of the effort once the experience has been digested. The Imperial War Museum is a case in point. Brilliant! I'm glad I persevered that day, it was worth the tube rides and having to cross the threshold into London.

I did get distracted for a while at the Mauer. A group of American tourists, well, two in particular. Callum and John, yes, I remember their names, their monickers garnered not through eavesdropping, but the name tags emblazoned across their chests. Why these were required, I'm not sure, given they were all in the same party and seemed to be known to one another. The group as a whole definitely weren't strangers. Judging by their attire, they were members of some golf club or the like. They looked like golfers, anyway. Stereotypical American seniors, all checked trousers and pastel coloured polo shirts. Sweaters inexplicably draped over the shoulders, loosely knotted. The female members, straight out of the hairdressers, new 'do's' obscured by peaked poker visors, pleated skirts of the cream variety and to use their parlance, blindingly white 'sneakers'.

Anyhow, I digress. Callum and John. They were arguing over a word. Was it real? Neither seemed entirely convinced, although each were positioned on the opposite side of a metaphorical wall. When in Berlin...

A right pair of tartan clad ne'er-do-wells! Well hardly. A bit harsh. I just like that saying. The word? 'Intertwangled'.

It sounded like it could be a word, familiar, just slightly off. I was on the fence, decided I'd have to look it up at some point. I caught myself stepping forward a pace, to join in with the discussion. John guided me away, pointing at nothing in particular, by way of a distraction, which I was grateful for.

"Didn't want you getting intertwangled," he muttered under his breath.

In the wee hours of the following morning, we wandered alone within the 'Schinkel Pavillon', John having persuaded the lone security chap that it would be a good idea to grant us access to his domain. They often think that they are the gatekeepers, masters of all they survey, these uniformed janitors. I suppose they are, and have to think like that. If they don't take responsibility for the security of those precious treasures contained within, who will? Certainly not the curator. He or she was probably fast asleep after a busy day big-wigging and the like. Don't ask me how John inveigled, yes, that's a real word, the fellow: 'I know nothing', to quote Sergeant Schultz.

Peter certainly was a talent, not only in the diplomatic sphere. I could have spent hours admiring his creations. Willpower straining at the leash, determined to comply with the 'Don't touch' signs. As dawn broke, we strode out of the museum, pausing to say our farewells to our uniformed benefactor. I'd observed John handing over a generous gratuity, and with that we'd put our best feet forward.

It was time for our next port of call. How were we intending to reach Frohburg? I won't dignify that with an answer. I'm sure you can guess by now. It did set me to thinking, though. Here I was spending hours on end aboard trains, planes and automobiles. Why was that? I knew fine well by now, the reason? John Willis of course, I was very much the junior member of this partnership. John did and quite rightly take the lead on most matters, particularly methods of transport. I'm not complaining, however, when I think of all those years spent fantasising about a personal teleport device, the better to avoid the maddening crowds, yet there sat I.

Not much I could do about that for now, unless, just maybe. If I kept my head down, reeled in the incessant questions, one day I might just be the proud owner of my own personal portal! It could happen, couldn't it? For the time being, I'll just think about the positives, the last few days. Yes, Berlin! I would return.

Auf Wiedersehen Berlin, nächster halt Frohburg!

FROHBURG

Next stop, yes, but the final episode of our Road Racing News adventure. It was the last round of this season's International Road Racing Championships, a time to decide who would wear the crown, who would go away disappointed, but determined to take that next step when battle resumed the following year.

There was a contrast in atmosphere. One you could cut with a knife emanating from those camps who still had a say in the outcome of the various title races. The other feeling was from those who were ready to party, once the serious business had been decided. A time to kick back and release that pent up tension, have a few beers with the team and opponents alike.

The fans were seemingly unaffected by these two opposing emotion-clouds, cheering on their favourites as you'd expect. Nothing overtly partisan in pure road racing though. If someone does well, the consensus is that it was well deserved. All are applauded from first to last; it takes a lot of bottle to do what they do and a great deal of sacrifice from those that get them on the grid in the first place.

Although I felt in a party mood, a last day of school feeling, there was still a sense of determination, to take the job seriously and produce the best report I could manage. The whole Bulgaria thing? It barely crossed my mind. There was nothing I could do now: wasted energy worrying about it. John never mentioned it and seemed as committed about his photography as I was about my writing. I fell into step with his aura of professional calm. So, it was all business during the day and the letting down of hair as the sun set. Not that I could spare much, partnered with John in his current form, we were both folically challenged, albeit, his lack out of choice.

It may have been September, but the darkness of night drew in slowly. Hazy red sunsets, smoke from sizzling sausages, the accompanying fried onions smell wafting across the paddock. I felt that at any moment I would levitate and float directly to the source, like Shaggy and Scooby on the trail of some delicious, aromatic snack.

I'd chosen an unoccupied picnic table and had set up 'camp' for the evening. Bratwurst, Krug of cold beer, my woodbine tin and phone. I was content to people watch. John wandered off here and there, taking candid shots with his camera. I think he really enjoyed photography, because none of these behind-the-scenes images would make it into Road Racing News. Engrossed he may have been, but I wasn't completely abandoned. He would return at just the right time to replenish my idiot juice.

Here is an example of my observations, for your delectation. Say that three times fast after a few jugs of German lager! Wait, if you're sporting a set of dentures, please ignore my challenge. It could be lethal for innocent bystanders. Two bare-chested bronzed Adonises... well, let's just say they liked their food and beer. Verbal sparring at the Bratwurst stand. In this neck of the woods, they probably call it 'Wilhelm waving'. The pair of them weren't stupid, well-rounded intellects, to match their bellies. I thought to myself, if you're clever, naturally intelligent, don't argue about the small, mundane things. Stuff you can't affect or simply can't be bothered to. Don't flex your head muscle on such matters. Think, and if you insist on pontificating, get stuck into the big questions. You won't stand a chance of affecting these either, but you'll at least give the little grey cells a thorough workout. Get those clever little neurons darting hither and thither like a swarm of tadpoles frantically looking for Mum and Dad.

John Willis interjected, mentally, 'Correct!'

My mind wandered off on a tangent. I wondered, was that how the German flag was imagined? Ketchup and mustard wrapped round a barbecue blackened bratwurst?

'Big thoughts indeed!' John again.

'Shurrup! and be gone from my swede!'

John returned to my temporary base camp, this time sporting matching Krugs. Before I could protest, he placated me. "This one's for me, Whiskers. If you can't beat them, join them, besides I like that slightly fuzzy, giddy feeling."

"Can you get drunk then? With your anatomy or whatever's going on in there." I drunkenly pointed my middle digit at his stomach, something off with my depth perception. "Whoops, sorry about that, John." I apologised as he regained his balance from my finger attack.

He laughed uproariously. Had he been off taking pictures or lashing it up on the sly? Good for him! The band in the adjacent marquee started to play, no techno or death metal or whatever. I didn't know exactly what I expected, but familiar-sounding soft rock anthems paired perfectly with the convivial atmosphere on that warm September night.

And then the unexpected happened. John rose from the bench, took a slurp of his beer… and, wait for it. He began to dance!

All action from the waist down, James Brown slidy moves. The upper body, the polar opposite. Stiff backed, to attention. You could imagine John drinking tea from a cup and saucer, pinky finger extended horizontally. I love a boogie and was tempted to join him, but I wouldn't have been able to properly observe his impressively entertaining display. Front row seats, who knows if the likes will ever be seen again, in my lifetime anyway?

The band took five, John slid sideways, spun, sat and lifted his beer mug in one fluid movement, drawing admiring looks from nearby ladies and envious frowns from the men. Me? I stood, infinitely less gracefully and offered up an equally uncoordinated round of applause. John let me carry on for a couple of claps longer than socially acceptable, then gently shoulder pressed me back to the seating position.

"Enjoyed that!"

"I could tell. Nice moves, John!"

"Thank you. A great way to lose yourself in the moment. All about rhythm and timing, yet the actual passage of time loses all relevance."

That was the highlight of the weekend, for me, anyway.

Monday morning, fresh, sun rising, shining brightly. Too bright for these eyes. Tone it down, Sol! Back at the bench, five minutes of shared quietude, slurping tentatively on piping hot coffee in between appreciative bites of an extremely generous bacon roll. They must have had to use up their stock before they tore everything down. Half a pig was in this one!

I broke the fast and initiated a debrief. In the background, the temporary village was being dismantled. Slower than usual, hangovers must have abounded. Not quite in time-lapse fashion, but not the usual frenetic pace. This was the end of the season for most. No rush to get on the road, caterers, merchandisers and race teams alike. Winter was coming.

We both had a shared love for this sport of ours, one that at times can be exhilarating, and on the other hand, can be unforgiving and cruel. I asked John what his thoughts were, explaining that I sometimes felt a sense of guilt when things went wrong.

He reassured me that I should feel no guilt. "Whether we, collectively," he spread his arms to encompass the other fans milling about, "were here or not, racing would continue. Don't they say the first race happened the moment the second bike was built? Or was it automobiles? The point stands. Humans thrive on competition, it's why you're at the top of the food chain, not consigned to history like the dinosaurs. The fact that these races survive, gives me hope. Keeps your evolutionary foot in the door. You see, Whiskers, in this period of history, we live in an unheroic age. Is this, is that allowed? It's refreshing. It may not seem so, but thankfully, these periods come and go, cyclical."

"Moto-cyclical?"

John sighed, but the point was taken, by me.

I took my opportunity to segue, no! not those daft two wheeled things, into another topic. A question I had been dying, pardon the pun, to ask John since we first met. The subject of his mortality. John had briefly broached the subject in Prague, after his near miss with the tram, but obviously, me being me, I wanted to know more. Unusually, I didn't just come out with it, I could be a bit of a blurter at times, forgoing subtlety in search of an answer.

I asked him what he expected from the next leg of our journey, Bulgaria and the confrontation that was beyond doubt. Did he have any reservations, concerns about his own well-being? What was the plan? Was there one, or simply play it by ear? Then, true to form, I got down to brass tacks, blurting time.

"Can you die, John?"

He took it in his stride. Knowing me, he'd have most likely expected this question yonks ago. I mean I'd asked just about every other imaginable.

"No, Whiskers, I cannot die, because I've never really lived, in the conventional sense."

Okay, I thought, well, ask a simple question and all that. I'll keep chipping away though, don't you worry about that!

"As far as Bulgaria goes, we need to reconnoitre, work out a plan once we've garnered some intel. I may have gifts, but we still need to put the pieces together, to pinpoint exactly where this xeno is, the location of his command centre, lair, for want of a better word. He's shielded, wily, protected. I want us to be forearmed, prepared to counter any threat or perceivable attack. We have the location, but he's not holed up in a bedsit. I understand he's set up his home in the heart of a mountain, catacombs to be precise, and, young Whiskers, we're going to bury this devious creature. One way…"

"Or the other! When do we strike?"

"No time like the present. We need to get you home and even I could do with a relax, a cat nap or three."

ROTTEN TO THE CORE

Well, here we were, Bulgaria. Sofia to be precise. It seemed like I'd been stretched from fingers to toes on a tanning frame, metaphorically. No, nothing to do with fake tans, those things they use to stretch and dry animal hides with.

These last few months I must have been to all four corners of the globe! Hadn't I? Well, at least two of them. Funny saying that, I mean, does a globe even have corners? I mean, it's round, isn't it? Spherical.

Come to mention it. Oh no! Here we go again, Whiskers and his blooming questions. Just one more, I've started so I'll finish. Where exactly do we go, travel, whenever we use these portal things? I'm not complaining, mind, I just wondered what path we travel. I bet it's very sciencey, one of those time and space types of an answer. I'd best not pester John with my nonsense for now, later though, remind me.

We hadn't bothered to book a hotel this time. John didn't want us to just go through the motions. This wasn't a working holiday like our previous journalistic jaunts, he wanted us on our toes, focused.

Yes, the opposition, if not at first, now knew more or less what we were up to and most definitely knew the location of our ultimate destination. Well, that's where 'he' was, wasn't it? Given all that, we didn't want to make it any easier on our watchers. Being half a step ahead was better than none.

I suggested we demur luxury, hotel-wise and opt for something more low-key. Somewhere clean and functional, no temptation to lounge about, enveloped, hugged into apathy by oversized armchairs and the like. We should be up and about early, beating the roll-call, ready to rock.

John enjoyed his luxuries, the comforts afforded by staying in the more up-market accommodations.

Me, I couldn't give a monkey's. As long as it was clean, had a bar and they didn't cheap out on the cooked breakfast.

We'd booked into Hotel Downtown, by no means a hostel. A lovely place, with some nice features, and yes, it had a bar. I'm talking about the pleasing stained glass in the lobby. I think it was aimed at business types given the clientele I observed walking briskly to and fro from either one of the on-site conference suites. Walking at such a pace obviously gave off an air of importance and control in some circles. Looked like they were desperate for the toilet, but didn't want to show it. A sign of 'businessy' weakness, not bladder perhaps.

True to our word, we were up bright and early. We convened in the breakfast room before all the suits turned up. Best to avoid their meeting rituals, briskly darting back and forth along the plentiful buffet, keeping a close eye on the choices of those higher up the food chain, and following suit accordingly, desperate for an approving nod or raised fork salute from across the table.

We set off for a leg-stretch round the streets of Sofia,

spending an hour wandering aimlessly, with cursory glances at various points of interest.

Unable to commit to any serious touristy stuff, we each must have been on the lookout for a watering hole. The streets had started to fill, workers, coffee containers brandished in out-stretched hands, the various logos apparently denoting some type of status level.

So, as soon as the Thirsty Dragon came into view, a collective 'ahh' was heard.

No communication required as we stepped off the curb in tandem, destination agreed.

As we sat in the leafy courtyard contemplating our slightly early beverages, lager for me, Irish coffee for John, I shattered the silence, not an observation, yet another question.

"John, what do you see, when you look around you, in Sofia, busy places in general?"

He raised an eyebrow, given the secluded area we found ourselves in, nevertheless he humoured me.

"Picture a scene not unlike Lowry's 'Coming from the Mill'. That's what I see, but roughly half the people are living, as in mortal beings. The rest are in shadow, the recently passed, the confused, pitiful creatures, innocents. Hiding in plain sight, to me, the various ne'er-do-wells, demonic foot soldiers, parasites. Not forgetting a number of our prey, the interlopers."

"Really? These demons, aliens… abundant, are they?" I thought to myself, I wish I could see what John sees, or do I?

John snapped me out of this vicious cycle.

"Wish, wish, wish! Stop wishing your life away. Concentrate on your strengths, improve the areas where you excel. Don't over compensate for the weaknesses. There will always be someone bigger, stronger, wiser, faster than you. Why not be a better you? Forget the rest."

He wasn't annoyed, you understand, just reading the signs that I was about to embark on a track, tying myself into knots. Now was not the time.

He continued, a more conciliatory tone the better to affirm his lack of annoyance. "Whiskers, you have gifts, talents. Those tailored to your unique character. Over these past few months, you've seen them bloom and equally as important, they're now underpinned by experience. Who knows what abilities you'll develop in the future. And hold onto this, you wouldn't be here, by my side if I didn't value and rely on your contribution. Don't forget, I might be able to view the xenos when in the immediate vicinity, but it's you who are clearly more gifted in that department. You're no charity case, Whiskers, basket case maybe."

He grinned and returned to his drink, content in his examination of the froth, tentative slurps. I doubted the red-hot liquid could affect him though. Stop, stop! No more wonderings. Roll a woodbine. Enjoy your beer, I admonished myself.

A few drinks, a spot of lunch and we re-traced our steps. Back to the hotel, a nap apiece, followed by a delicious dinner in the hotel restaurant. I didn't pester John with any 'are we there yet, Dad?' type questions. I'd be ready when he was. At this stage I didn't need to know about mights and maybes: they added zero value. John retired to bed and I ordered a final beer. A woodbine out front, on the hotel steps and, resisting a final, final lager, I headed upstairs.

The day had been relaxed, calming, by design, I'd concluded. That was the intention anyway, however I'd experienced a sense of unease throughout. From time-to-time I'd see fleeting shadows in the corner of my eye. I always take those seriously, not to be nonchalantly brushed off. On more than one occasion I'd felt the sensation of spider webs brushing across my face.

If you've ever inadvertently walked through a cobweb in a dusty old shed, you'll no doubt sympathise. It's more than dis-comfort, a yuck moment to me though. It's another warning, a type of paranormal alarm. John had acted quickly when I showed signs of wandering, losing focus. Well, it worked. I wasn't anxious about what lay ahead. I was, however on high alert but remarkably duly entered the land of nod, not hearing more than a couple of chapters of my latest audiobook. My usual dream fest was notable in its absence. The night wasn't without incident though.

At three in the morning, I nearly leapt out of bed, instead performing a scissor kicking motion which resulted in a sore foot and a lamp going for a flight across the room, thankfully avoiding any further damage. The cause of my Bruce Lee impression? A flashing image of a multi-eyed hideous creature peering towards me as if attempting to unlock my mind, the accompanying soundtrack a mixture of high-pitched, ear-drum assaulting clicks and scratches. It dissipated as rapidly as it had appeared, but whoever was behind it had failed to achieve the effect they most likely desired. In such situations, fear is not my first, second or third reaction. I feel anger, controlled I should point out. Despite the resultant lamp attack! I channel that initial feeling into determination and a will to fight back, not allowing myself to be intimidated.

Groundhog Day, well, bacon roll morning anyway. Offerings demolished, second cup of tea on the go. John leapt to his feet emitting a James Brown-esque yowl, startling a passing waiter, temporarily affecting his elegant gait. Anticipating my questioning look. I was going to enquire if it was dancing hour. John produced one of his patented twirls and landed back on his seat, chin balanced on tented forefingers, staring mischievously across the divide. I was busy thinking that this impromptu display reminded me of the cat from Red Dwarf and that Danny John-Jules was also a big bike fan. The expectant questioning from me not forthcoming, he'd emitted a mini screech, mindful that one of the chefs was replenishing the baked beans. Eyes sparkling, pupils expanding before… my eyes, he excitedly declared, "Let's do this thang!"

I was good to go. A quick brush of the teeth and I headed back down to the lobby. A cheeky smoke outside and John joined me on the steps of the hotel entrance. He'd informed his new friend on the front desk that we'd be gone for a couple of nights at most and there was no need to bother with housekeeping. John had built up a rapport with various key members of the hotel staff. I noted this down, mentally. It's always handy to have allies as a stranger abroad, whether you're embarking on an important mission to save humanity or not.

A taxi pulled up and John jumped in the front, me consigned to the back. No complaints there. The two up front appeared to know each other, not at the level of the desk clerk, something deeper.

I presumed it was some contact or colleague. Besides, it would have been strange if he'd chosen any old taxi/driver combination.

We were heading for Tsarichina, not far, a nature reserve about an hour's drive north of Sofia. John and the driver were busy chatting away, the music from the radio just loud enough so I couldn't quite catch what they were waffling on about.

All I could hear were the 'S' sounds of individual words. Trust me once you hear them, it's hard to filter them out. You'll hear this phenomenon on a busy bus. Careful, though, as it's amplified ten-fold compared to a taxi. All you can hear is a nails-on-chalkboard symphony of S's. It's like you're sharing the bus with thirty snakes on some works' outing to the seaside. Excitedly hissing about their day ahead, glad to be out of the ladders factory while the chutes are being refurbished. Long overdue… Sssss.

We came to a halt in the village of Tsarichina. I don't know how these things are classified, but it was that small it must have only just made the cut from… whatever is smaller than a village. Ahh! A hamlet, though this one had a church. We got out next to it. Looked like it was of the Orthodox variety. The architecture will be familiar to those who've travelled across the Baltic states.

John was theatrically stretching his legs and arching his torso backwards. He looked like John Cleese from Fawlty Towers. I took the opportunity to lean in through the still open passenger door.

"Thank you for the lift."

The driver was in mid chomp of a large red apple. He swallowed, winked, made a hissing noise. Darted his tongue side to side and seeing the reaction on my face, laughed uproariously. It was obviously contagious because I joined in too, realisation of his meaning dawning on me.

I stepped back and waved farewell as he sped off back from whence he came, dispersing or taking half of the dirt parking area with him.

I noticed a solitary curtain twitch from the scattering of houses as we crossed over the road and down a nearby farm track. Although they must be used to paranormal adventurers in this neck of the woods, it must have still disturbed the tranquillity, especially when accompanied by raucous laughter and Colin McRae rally car impressions, although, I'm sure it only elicited a raised eyebrow at most, before he or she returned to their distraction of choice, TV show, knitting or whatever.

"What was that driver's name?" I asked John.

"Adam."

"Well, why doesn't that surprise me...?"

"Bit of an asp really, ha! No, he's a good egg, we go back a long, long way."

As soon as we left the dirt track and entered the forest proper, John took on his favoured cat form, albeit this time, a scaled-up version. He must have been four times the size of your average cat. He assured me that this was purely for practical reasons, not aesthetics or some pitiful attempt to intimidate. It afforded him a better field of view in these denser forested areas.

"Besides, I prefer this size." He stood up on hind quarters fore-paws rubbing up and down his body, by way of illustrating the point. Imagine trying to smooth one of those ruffled dress shirts by running your palms up and down, elbows tight. Finishing with a hands out, or paws in this case, gesture. As if visiting a palm reader who was offering a buy one, get one free deal…

"I rarely get the opportunity back in England. It tends to cause alarm, and local TV news jump all over these types of stories, spreading panic and directing unwanted attention my way. You must have heard of the Beast of Bodmin Moor, down in Cornwall? That type of story. The sightings have been going on for decades now. And before you ask, no comment."

We resumed our walk. Pleasant, really: nice warm day, fresh air and exercise. I was sure the forest would take on a whole different persona once the night fell though.

I felt a change in the atmosphere, like the air had stilled, the soundtrack of the area extinguished in an instant. Like we were in a bubble, the world carrying on outside as per usual. John had noticed the change perhaps a second before me. Doesn't sound long, does it? But it's all relative. Imagine if you knew a sniper was going to shoot at you a second before their brain sent a message to the trigger finger. Aware he may have been, but he didn't seem unduly worried. Do cats ever, though?

Something similar to a portal appeared, this one flat to the forest floor. I glanced at John. He shook his head. This wasn't of his doing. The portal thing must have measured eight feet across, or so. It slowly irised open to reveal a rather plain set of stairs, spiralling and descending down to who knows where.

"Well, there's only way to find out." John echoed my thoughts. "Ready?"

"Let's do this!" I declared.

We put our best foot and paw forward, green panel lights waking from their slumber and illuminating the walls as we descended deeper. I didn't notice the portal door thing close, but did ponder that judging by its diameter and the width and depth of the stairs, the resident creature could be of humanoid dimensions. I soon put that out of my mind, reasoning that this structure could have been appropriated. Anyway, for all I knew this was the tradesman's entrance.

Besides, this wasn't the time for speculation. This was real, not one of those conspiracy documentaries, desperately trying to be taken seriously, whilst being hosted by a loon with an inexplicably large forehead and equally ridiculous bouffant, 'high hair', dressed for the occasion by some wardrobe attendant who must sprinkle magic mushrooms on his breakfast cereal of choice.

So, I followed John as we continued our journey of discovery, the temperature rising, pleasant though, basking, not burning-type heat. I was trying to open up my senses, controlling my fight or flight instincts, choosing another option, awareness, the spatial variety.

Of course, the two more traditional options were still firmly placed on the table. I just wanted to slow down my personal time, the better to make informed decisions should it come to legging it or striking out first, asking questions later.

Sensing my unease, John wrapped his tail gently around my leg. He was a few hands taller in current form though, and that furry snake wrapped around my thigh initially evoked the opposite of what was intended. Pleasingly my first reaction was to leap to one side and ready a strike! Good to know I wasn't prepared to high-tail it out of the joint, at the first sign of danger. The next emotion to surface was an overwhelming desire to laugh uproariously. I suppressed and downgraded it to a muffled giggle, John joining in on the action. Ice broken, we regained our composure and descended further into what I figured was the belly of this hollowed out mountain.

The last illuminated wall panel had triggered as we stepped into an Albert Hall sized cavern, hewn out of the mountain rock, not roughly, though, the walls smooth, jet black. Not highly polished, more of a satin finish. You could see yourself reflected, but a slightly out-of-focus representation. From the ceiling protruded stalactites of a similar hue to the walls. Intimidating, needle sharp looking and not worth the effort of counting. I wasn't sure whether these were natural or not, given the colour, not that it made any difference.

That part of the cavern was illuminated by some type of flickering wall torches. It was hard to make out, but I discerned they weren't of the open flame variety, you know, like you'd imagine a medieval dungeon would sport. They were most likely a modern take on them, though. You could say they were a bit tacky, yet infinitely more practical. John was striding ahead, loping, or whatever the terminology. His feline eyesight leaps and bounds ahead of my ocular capabilities. He'd obviously picked up on this lacking and a beautiful white light enshrouded him, guiding me forward. I quickly caught up and joined him by his side.

The light emanating from John grew, spreading out in a circle across the cavern floor. It was as if we were on stage, illuminated from a lighting rig situated somewhere up in the rafters. I could feel the spiritual power of this personal beacon of his, it's hard to explain. It was a dichotomy, yes, I had to look that up. It was on the tip of my tongue though, honest guv'nor. It felt both powerful and comforting at the same time. You wouldn't want to be on the receiving end if you didn't measure up; if you were deemed worthy of protection, you were golden!

I shuffled to my left to step into the edge of the light. John held up a paw. I stopped in my tracks and gazed in wonder as a similar but less impressive version started to expand around me. This flickering cloak of light was coming from within me.

John hadn't gifted it to me, siphoned off a bit of his. This was me! He'd just helped trigger the release of something hitherto dormant. Some sort of extension of my aura, I figured, as I grew used to the idea and just accepted it. As a result, the light strengthened and the flickering ceased. No need to change the bulb, then!

John slowed to a halt, this light of his moving slowly forward and up, revealing the far wall of the chamber. The central panel of the wall was basked in light. On the outer edges of this inner area were crystals jutting out at all angles, no particular order; all shapes and sizes vying for dominance, breathing space at a premium. John narrowed the diameter of his light, focusing his beam, closing in on the epicentre of the wall. I, getting the hang of things, followed suit, earning a nod of affirmation from John.

A spider-being encased in a web-patterned crystal cocoon was revealed. It looked massive, at least a 12ft span from outstretched leg-to-leg. Its torso, jet black, the size of a sailor's duffle bag. This wasn't an exact representation of what we would think a spider should look like. That's why I said torso. It was as if a tall, thin human with an oversized head had decided that two legs and arms just wouldn't cut the mustard so he'd doubled up. The head was equally as convoluted and creepy as the spider equivalent though. All eye clusters and fangs. Looked over-engineered to me. The unwanted visitor, the flashing image I'd experienced the previous night back in Sofia, one and the same I realised.

That's it! He, I presumed, looked like that Vitruvian

Man drawing by Leonardo de Vinci, albeit after some precocious kid had added a few scary bits with his crayons.

"Gashkara Pak-Nar Namood!" the creature boomed from within his crystalline prison, the sound echoing up and down the chamber, slowly dissipating.

John was seen to stagger back a step or two. I was unaffected by what I presumed was a magical incantation of sorts. John seemingly regained his composure, making a show of locking his hind legs as he raised himself up on them.

What next? I thought, bracing myself, attempting to strengthen my personal light. I wasn't sure quite how, but soon found myself distracted by John. Standing erect, paws on hips, he threw back his head and burst out into laughter. Initially shocked, I soon joined in, contagious as it was.

Paws now resting on bended knees, his back arched forward, he struggled valiantly to regain his composure. The creature seemed content to wait on this process. As the echoes of guffaws ebbed away, he continued, seemingly undeterred.

"You think you can defeat me by resolve alone? With nothing more than the power of your pathetic excuse for a mind?"

John interrupted him, sensing the impending diatribe that the spider being had most likely been rehearsing for some time.

"No, I'll defeat you due to the weakness of yours, zero imagination, no moral compass, only emptiness, pathetic avarice, a carcass, a chasm of nothingness. How do you like them apples?"

"I don't understand the meaning of… them apples."

"You wouldn't. No imagination, see?"

"You talk in riddles, my head hurts!" whined the creature.

John mind-messaged me. 'That light of yours, direct it towards matey, project thoughts of love, pity and forgiveness. You don't actually love him, that'd be weird. Just bombard him with positivity, higher thoughts.'

'Understood,' I lied.

'I'm going to wind him up and confuse him. You do understand, Whiskers, you've directed similar healing thoughts to yourself and others in the past.'

'Oh yeah! Duh.' Have I?

John's light dimmed, appearing to lose its resolve. The spider-being, seemingly emboldened and fixated on this apparent success, failed to notice the strengthening of my light as he embarked on a poison tongued rant. He hated this, he wanted to destroy that. His race would rule over the remnants of these pitiful creatures that John ill-advisedly chose to protect. Those greedy, weak, off-world species that have cosied up to their equally greedy human counterparts and interfered with his plans would get their come-uppance too. I got on with my thought attack or whatever it's called, love shower? Nah! Sounds creepy. I still managed to follow the creature's tirade though, keen to hear John's riposte.

John was biding his time. Evidently employing his favoured tactic, give them enough rope and all that.

Old Eight-legs was embarking on another verbal attack. He blamed John and his fellow winged do-gooders for imprisoning him, here, in the first place. Mocking these angelic busy-bodies, boasting about the ease in which he'd managed to create a network of agents, ultimately luring John and his gormless protégé to their doom. It didn't bother me. Been called worse.

"Revenge is a dish best served pre-emptively!" declared the creature.

"What? That makes no sense whatsoever!" replied John, quizzically.

"Yes… it… I, I meant… you don't under…"

"You're an idiot."

"You'll regret that!" threatened old spider features.

"Later? Or before…? Pre-emptively perhaps?"

"SCREIGNOTT!!"

John turned towards me. "I think he loves me."

He tilted his head to one side, amused. An image appeared in my mind, John munching on popcorn, you're doing great, keep going, was the message. The creature's focus followed suit and he directed his attention to me.

"Yours is a race of diseased vermin!"

I interrupted, my face a picture of bored disinterest. "Write a letter," I advised.

John quick to realise that I'd entered the ring, unnoticed by old six-eyes, began to amp up his light, white developing into scarlet at the edges.

"Wha… write a… what?"

"You heard!"

"Why on Kalsek would I write a letter?"

"Well, it's definitely the thing to do if you want to be taken seriously." I adopted a condescending tone as if to humour an errant child. "Or are you just ranting, venting?"

"Well... no... I... um. I'm serious!" Poised to recommence his rant, limbs straining against the confines of his imprisonment.

I repeated my advice. "Write a letter then."

We ceased further discourse, leaving him to fume, metaphorical smoke pouring out of his ears, head holes or whatever. John's light changed shape, forming an orb that enveloped him, no prison this. Protective, weaponised it had begun pulsating bright red on the surface, brilliant white at the core. I kept my light a polite distance from John's. I hadn't completely fathomed it out yet, I didn't want to disrupt the fields or reverse the polarity. It sounded plausible, must have seen it on a Star Trek episode. The spider being cottoned on too late, now caught up in a different type of web, a malaise of hatred and confusion.

A point of light shot out from within John's orb. A great sense of love, hope and positive emotions washed over me, nearly knocking me off my feet. This angelic radiation was just the outer edges of the force that had been directed at our xenophobic nemesis. It pierced the crystal that up to now had both imprisoned and offered a certain amount of protection to the creature, pieces bursting outwards in a shower of light-refracting detritus.

I had instinctively ducked and dived. No need. My

light-protection dealt easily with the deadly-looking crystalline shrapnel.

Undaunted, the scarlet bayonet of light drove deeper into the creature's chest.

For such a being, so full of hate and bile, it was overwhelming. To let so much love and positivity into his soul was far beyond his ken. His body's reaction was immediate and the prognosis wasn't favourable, for him. Convulsing, screaming, vibrating so rapidly he became a blur of agonised movement.

For all the drama, in such a short space of time, I'd failed to notice that the crystal encasement had greatly magnified the true nature of this physically intimidating creature. It plopped to the floor, broken, defeated.

John, having reverted to human form, fished about in his jacket. He retrieved a small box, and duly emptied the contents into his pocket. A match box, inscribed with the words 'Zorbas Taverna'! The now pitiful creature was unceremoniously deposited into this makeshift sarcophagus. No, wait, I was a bit previous. As John closed the tiny box, a pathetic voice emanated from within.

"You may have won this battle, but the war continues, John Willis! Others will follow, our network lives on… for I am just a node! A NODE!"

"More like a gonad!" John muttered as he slammed the box shut, well as best you can, made from cardboard as it was. Imprisoned once more, not quite as impressive a jail cell, but incarcerated nonetheless. John stepped two paces back and before him appeared a tea saucer sized green portal, into which he nonchalantly flung the creature into the abyss.

Unsolicited, John corrected my conclusions. "Scattered across space and time, Whiskers. Well, at least there'll be a period of peace and quiet in the neighbourhood, like getting rid of that noisy couple next door. Alas, the effect is only temporary."

"Not the end?"

"There is no end, Whiskers. The creature's physical body is no more, but his essence lives on. Maybe some sort of redemption will be proffered, in time. I doubt it though."

I rubbed my hands together. "What now, John? Home?"

A bit of a banal question given the events of the last hour, felt like sixty minutes, anyway. We'd dissect, maybe celebrate, later. It was all too fantastical to sum up with some glib statement or outpouring of emotion. I wanted to ground myself in the familiar. I'd reflect on things in my own time.

"I suppose we could teleport home, now. Where's the fun in that though? James Bond managed the odd break. Picture Ursula Andress emerging from the waves or off-piste enjoying a spiced rum in a snow-covered lodge, roaring fire. Skiing? Not for me though, no thank you. Two oversized lollipop sticks strapped to your feet, pointy litter picking poles in either hand. The Ursula option please. Anyway, the point being, we deserve a break before heading back. I need to digest today's happenings as well. Let's head back to Sofia. A couple of beers and I think you deserve a bit of Greek food after today, don't you?"

"Yeah, baby!" I shouted excitedly.

"Come on then, let's ditch this joint. Adam will be waiting for us."

"You pre-booked him? Got to admire your confidence!"

"Want to sit up front this time?"

"Not at all."

"Incidentally, Whiskers, I never had a doubt!"

FAIRY BRIDGE

We spent a couple more nights in Sofia, doing the touristy stuff, wining and dining. No dancing this time, thankfully.

True to his word, John treated me to a Greek at the aptly named Yamas restaurant. That means cheers in Greek and that particular word made an appearance on several occasions as we let our proverbial hair down. Disclaimer: No plates were harmed during the making of these hangovers.

All too soon, social fatigue caught up with me. I don't think John suffers from any type of weariness affliction. It was time to head home, well, not mine, John's.

I accompanied John as we portalled from Sofia to Heysham port, a couple of miles down the coast from Morecambe. I'd travelled to the Isle of Man from here a couple of times, to watch the TT. Why didn't we just portal direct to Douglas? Well, we both like the ferry and the Irish Sea was like a mill pond, for a change.

We didn't talk shop on the trip, just chilled and enjoyed the facilities on the 'Manxman'. It was my first experience of this particular ferry as it had only entered service the year before. John made use of the new onboard streaming service and I read my book.

The trip takes just under four hours, depending on the weather, how angry the sea is. In the blink of a few hundred eyes, it was time to gather our belongings, well mine. John doesn't bother himself with all that malarkey, just changes form, conjures up anything he needs. Within reason anyway, remember the camera I'd forked out for him? No matter. To me, money spent is money gone, no point worrying about. Not to say I won't mention it if he were to require taking down a peg or three.

As tradition dictated, we headed outside for the approach to Douglas port. Not quite as much freedom and variety of viewing spots as were available onboard the Ben-my-Chree, but it was what it was.

"Where are we going?" I enquired.

"Somewhere particular in mind?"

"Well, I still don't know whereabouts exactly you call home, here." The veiled inquiry went unanswered, so I continued. "I'd like to visit the Fairy Bridge. I never got round to it in the past. Oh, and Peel! I fancy a toasted sandwich in the Marine Hotel."

John, still in the human form he'd chosen in Sofia, a knowing smile forming on his face, stuffed his hands into jacket pockets and with the words, "Lead on, Macduff!" obviously not understanding or ignoring the essence of his call to arms, he strode off in search of a taxi. I was ahead of the game, though. I'd found a card in my rucksack, dating back to 2015. It was a beermat from the 'Rovers Return', no! not the Weatherfield version, with Barry Wood and a mobile number scribbled on the back.

Barry duly pulled up across from the ferry terminal and I managed to leap into the front passenger seat as John was executing a 180 degree turn.

"Where first, Whiskers?"

I could sense John failing to control a raised eyebrow.

"Fairy Bridge please."

"Which one?"

"The one just past Murray's Motorcycle Museum please, I know it's a bit of a faff but can you drop us off at the other one after?"

"Of course, it's your money, Whiskers," he chuckled.

Barry is a Manxman and a motorcycle racer, his Manx Grand Prix and TT career spanning three decades. He also happens to be a fantastic bloke. His knowledge and insight in relation to road racing is second to none, in my opinion, although true to form he's far too humble to entertain such a notion.

Regardless, I made the most of the ten minutes or so of the journey and proceeded to question his ears off. I wouldn't have blamed him if he'd dropped us off and got the hell out of there before I returned to renew my earhole assault on the next leg of our bridge-based sojourn. Instead of a Starsky and Hutch impression, he relaxed back in his seat and fished his paper out from the sun visor. "No rush!" he shouted after us.

It was only a few yards or so from where Barry had pulled in, so we soon arrived at bridge number one of the day. We observed the local tradition of greeting the fairies and John peered over the edge, elbows resting awkwardly on the parapet. Meanwhile, I was busy reading all of the little notes attached to a nearby tree trunk. There were pictures of visitors and racers alike, some faded beyond recognition, others attached only months prior.

I didn't see any shadowy outlines of figures like I'd observed in the Traf, that seemed like an age ago now. A lot of water had passed under the bridge since then, I mused, forgetting for a moment where I was. I did feel an energy though, not of the tranquil variety, of a place which is a focal point for outpourings of different emotions; this place, the touchstone for race fans wanting to offer protection to all who face their fears in an attempt at conquering, this, the greatest of all road racing courses.

We stood in silence for a moment and I said a small prayer to myself, in remembrance of the fallen.

We returned to the taxi and Barry dropped us off close to Kewaigue School. We said our farewells, paid the piper and set off in search of what's sometimes described as the real or original Fairy Bridge.

I'd been alerted to its existence having seen and read the description of a painting by my friend David. No, I won't disclose the location. If you're truly interested, you'll find out, like I did. There are ways and means, i.e. tap a few letters into your search engine of choice.

John knew where he was going, so I fell into step, I seem to do that a lot, and let him lead the way.

I'd watched a YouTube video which showed you the direction to take, so the majority of the scene was familiar to me.

This place had a completely different vibe, tranquil, that comforting feeling of protection when embraced by Mother Nature. Not quiet by any means, the countryside, streams are always a hive of activity, but this was peaceful in its own way, owing in part due to its location, this bridge set back from any road, off the beaten track.

I felt an energy. I guessed there was some type of portal here. I doubted it was your run-of-the-mill interdimensional gateway, the transit type portal that I'd grown accustomed to. This one was a direct route from some other realm: only one station stop on this line.

I imagined the souls of riders popping in and out, kindly fairy creatures seeing to their needs, welcoming back frequent visitors, offering words of comfort to those visiting for the first time.

I felt too embarrassed to share these fanciful notions with John. Maybe I wasn't that far from the truth. I mean, with all I'd experienced recently it wasn't beyond the bounds of possibility, was it?

It dawned on me that whether I was close to the mark or not was irrelevant. The fact remained, that this was a very special, idyllic space. If it offered some type of comfort, a place to grieve, pay your respects, to those who visited, it mattered not from where, or who chose this place to spend a quiet moment. And that's the bottom line! To coin a phrase.

John looked at his timepiece: he prefers that to 'watch'.

"Time to go, Whiskers, four minutes past ten."

A questioning look from John elicited a non-committal response from yours truly, a shrug.

We stepped away and set off back down the track.

"You wanted to know whether we'd make use of the bridge portal?" asked John.

"Yes."

"And if not, how were we going to get back to Peel?"

"Correct," I replied, sounding more like John Willis with each passing day.

"Well, as you no doubt will have worked out, maybe hypothesised, this particular portal is reserved for bridge visitors, not to be employed for general travel, therefore misuse is frowned upon unless in an emergency. We'll have a stroll towards Bradden and jump on a bus. Besides, the pubs aren't open yet!" Laughing jovially, he patted me on the back.

The toastie in the Marine was just as good as I'd remembered, no rose-tinted taste buds, thankfully. We had a mooch along the shore road, over the footbridge, towards the castle, and had a decko over the edge of the breakwater, hoping to see the seals. They must have been on a break, enjoying their equivalent of a toasted treat. We did an about-turn and headed back towards the quay side, stopping for a beverage in the Peveril, followed by the Creek Inn. It wasn't all melted cheese and alcohol though! There was a shot of culture thrown into the mix. We had a look round the Leece and House of Manannan museums. Incidentally I wouldn't recommend challenging John to say the latter three times fast after a few pints. He aced it, with flying colours. I shelved the 'Ken Dodd's dad's dog's dead' challenge… for now!

After a whirlwind, but fun-packed tour, we set off walking.

"Where are we heading, John?"

"We're off to my digs. I've told my landlady she'll have an extra guest for a couple of nights. Alright with you?"

"Yes, definitely. As long as she's okay with it. Told or asked?"

"Requested."

So, we walked, each step adding to a growing sense of familiarity.

As we headed out of Peel, John reverted to his cat form, of the normal sized variety.

Pop! His tail disappeared. "Got to fit in with the locals!" he declared.

I'm sure he could have just transformed with the tail edited out. Showing off! He heard my intentionally unshielded thoughts.

"Whimsy, Whiskers. Whimsy!" giving me a John Willis-patented wink.

Seemed in a jolly mood. Might try that Ken Dodd challenge after all, I thought.

"No chance!" came the reply.

Must shore up my mental defences: that one was definitely unintentional.

We passed through the parish of Patrick. We couldn't be, could we?

We were, you know! This was Gordon. You'd have difficulty finding it on the map. There's a bungalow on one side of the road, three Manx cottages and a detached house on the other.

I'd stayed here for the TT in 2015 and in 2017 Lisa had joined me for her first Tourist Trophy experience. They called it 'homestay', but basically, you're a short-term lodger. It's great value and takes the stress out of finding a hotel during a period when this small island is swamped with road racing fanatics.

The Stallards, my hosts, had gone above and beyond on both occasions, going out of their way, literally, to make my stay as enjoyable as possible.

I'm not keen on using that word... literally... it's redundant for the most part. "I'm literally at the end of the street." Well, you're at the end of the street then? "I'm literally bursting at the seams!" Mmmm I don't think you are... literally!

Anyway, enough of that.

They'd gone out of their way, by dropping us off in Peel, when their destination had been downtown Douglas. I'd been collected and poured into the back seat when I'd been here, there and everywhere enjoying myself after the roads had re-opened following practice, qualifying or race day.

We'd all been out for a meal at Niarbyl and on one occasion, they'd visited us in Scarborough, Paul and Andrea arriving in style aboard a steam train from Liverpool.

No wonder John had felt at home, Paul being a fellow train enthusiast.

I'm back. Sorry, I just went on a track there, pardon the pun. I wondered if there was a posh name for rail buffs. There is: 'Ferroequinologist' from the Latin words for iron and horse. Apologies. Now where was I?

Ah yes, in a nutshell, the Stallards were good people. I wondered where John had been during my previous visits, changed form to blend in? They had two Manx cats in residence, so that wouldn't have worked.

"John?"

"Oh that. Myself and a colleague had represented the other two guests that stayed here during your visits."

"No coincidence that the same two happened to stay here on both occasions then?"

A head tilt and grin, the only reply I'd be getting.

I persevered. "Okay then, how did you explain to the Stallards, your absence during the TT, given you're a racing fan?"

"Easy, I was helping out with one of the teams. Where better to be than the paddock?"

The household was obviously ruled over by the resident Manx cats. Humans are only ever guests as soon as a cat crosses the threshold, in their opinion anyway. I remember these two going bonkers after a session on the cat nip during my last visit. I'd have loved to see the effect on John. Would his cat form leave him vulnerable to such a manic possession? I doubt it. Fun to imagine, though, to picture the scene.

Paul and Andrea were shocked to hear I was having an early night, not the Whiskers they remembered from past exploits!

I promised that we'd all have a drink the following evening at the Whitehouse before I set off home. Appeased, I bid everyone goodnight and was out like a light. No weird dreams, waking during the witching hour, just a smooth transition from lights out to eyes open.

I was going to have a day to myself wandering around Peel. I'd declined the offer of a lift from Paul, I figured a walk would do me good after the hearty breakfast that Andrea had provided.

The walk did its job. I could feel the strain on my belt easing following every footfall, best tighten it up a notch before I risked arrest due to lewd behaviour! As I poised to adjust myself, a blooming branch came hurtling down, dealing a glancing blow to my bonce! Given my recent adventures, it was a timely reminder: not every unusual happening is necessarily of a paranormal nature.

I'd need to dial things back if I was going to return to my normal routine, life before John Willis. Well, my knowledge of his existence, anyway. He'd never been far, if not physically then mentally. That's what I gathered anyway. I'd have to drop the para, embrace the normal.

•

And so, it was the end of the road, for now at least. Me? This is John by the way. I'd returned to the Isle of Man, to my lodgings in Gordon. Whiskers? Oh, he was there too, well on the Isle of Man somewhere, probably daydreaming in some watering hole in Peel, the Royal if I was to hazard a guess. I'm not his keeper, impossible! Let's just describe me as a guardian of sorts, although that responsibility diminishes by the day, such is the pace of his development.

He'd accompanied me on this final leg, three legs. Ha! Talking of Manx symbols and the like! Why? Well, I thought it was about time he'd returned, he likes a ferry trip and I wanted him to experience the Fairy Bridge, develop his understanding. And so, having ticked those boxes and as the sun sets on this beautiful Isle, it's a good night from me and goodnight from him. Hang on, getting ahead of myself, best conjure up some dapper garb: we were all heading out for a farewell drink. Then it'll be the goodnight speech, on the other hand just take it as read.

•

I'd taken advantage of the morning culinary delights offered up by Andrea and having said my goodbyes, it was time to make a move. John accompanied me to the waterfall at Glen Maye in order to open a portal for my trip back to Scarborough.

"I really must instruct you in the use of these things at some point."

"Can't you just gift me the knowledge?"

"No, it's a bit more convoluted than that, Whiskers, transit protocols, red tape of a fashion. Besides, where's the satisfaction in that? Learn by doing. No app available for this network, my friend."

As we were about to carry out our farewell rituals, we were interrupted by a portal preparing to stabilise and establish an opening, out of which stepped a rather striking, golden-haired fellow.

John greeted our visitor. "Ah Michael! Long time no see."

"I see you've been busy. How should I address you, still going by John Willis? Anyway, the big man is impressed. He says there might well be hope for you yet. He likes surprises, makes him feel almost human, fallible."

"As he often says…" The pair of them reciting in harmony, "Nobody likes a know it all!"

"Goodbye John…"

"Michael."

He, this Michael, turned to me, smiled and produced a shallow bow of the head.

And with that he stepped into the portal and was off.

"Well," John declared in an amused tone. "That was Michael."

"The Michael?"

"Yes, Whiskers, The Michael. We are honoured." Only a hint of sarcasm detected.

We shook hands, he squeezed my shoulder. Unlike me, John isn't a natural-born hugger.

"Go on, Whiskers, no time like the present. Lisa and Winnie will be wondering where you are. The Traf's takings will be down too. You'd best do something about it."

We both snorted and I was home, emerging from the portal set within the grounds of Dean Road cemetery.

I strode out of the shadows. Stopping to stroke my chin… hmm, equidistant from home and the Traf, bit of a quandary. What to do?

As I headed towards Murchison Street, I decided on a compromise.

"Come on, you two!" I declared as I came bursting

through the door. "Let's go for a lady and gentleman!" That's our code for a quiet drink and debrief in a beer garden somewhere on Falsgrave.

Lisa and Winnie needed no persuasion so we spent a couple of hours chatting and laughing, as we do. I told her some of what had occurred since I'd seen her last, Lisa bringing me up to date on domestic affairs, Winnie looking at us with mock disapproval.

'Silly humans, drinking their equally silliness-inducing beverages! Well, there better be something in it for me! Cheese or gammon trim, no! Both! Woof!' thought Winnie.

It was good to be home.

BACK TO LIFE, BACK TO REALITY

There hadn't been any pressing need for me to make the Isle of Man trip. I didn't want to just decelerate from 100mph to zero, I wanted to ease back into semi-retirement. Who knew when I'd see or hear from John again. Was my role as an international man of mystery over?

I very much doubted that, the creature in the cave had said he was only a node, as he put it, shortly before being flushed down the naughty boy's toilet to who knows where. I was under no illusions, if he was indeed just a node, part of a network of adversaries, then the peace could surely only be of the temporary variety.

I'd also wanted to visit the Isle of Man following a hiatus of seven years, meet the Stallards again, and the real Fairy Bridge had been on my mind for at least the last four years.

John and I also had a few loose ends to tie. We'd sorted these out prior to our evening out with Andrea and Paul, the two of us forming a recce party and heading to the Royal in Peel. We'd arranged to meet the Stallards at seven'ish. This gave us a couple of hours secreted in the secluded beer garden to the rear of my favourite Isle of Man pub.

And so, we discussed various items on the agenda, agreed on what actions to take, or not, as the case may be.

Albert had proved himself useful to John, apparently. No longer a flight risk, ha! He'd come under John's jurisdiction from here on in. Luna and Lola would be stood down as soon as 'Albatross' arrived back home. A double agent no longer, I imagined he'd be doing bits and bobs of field work for John. Nothing too critical, risky. I think John had developed a soft spot for the gentleman.

Trevor would continue to watch over Oliver's Mount, maintain the peace. A nice team forming, new contacts spanning the length and breadth of Europe.

"But what of me?" I'd asked.

John was non-committal; maybe he, too, was in the dark, waiting for instructions, from his higher-ups, that Michael fellow perhaps? I was to continue my development, get back into my routine. He'd be in touch from time to time, whether it be for business or pleasure. I hoped so. Maybe I'd give it a month or two on the work front though. It'd be race-season in the blink of an eye, or two.

Concerns assuaged, we'd enjoyed a pleasant night, the four of us.

I'd been home for a couple of weeks, back into my routine by now. Shopping at the indoor market for Mum on Thursdays, followed by her 'beaking' assault when I dropped the provisions round. I call it that when ladies talk ten to the dozen, at you. I don't have the necessary software installed within. I can't compress the dialogue file, convert it into a legible language.

I lose track of what I'd planned on discussing. It's

of a completely different frequency to man talk, which is more akin to a couple of chimpanzees grunting and screeching at one another, albeit without the associated shared grooming and bottom inspections, not in the circles I move in anyway. Each to their own though, inspect away if it's your bag.

I'd been writing some notes and had tentatively started work on a new project: a biography about a motorcycle racer who'd competed at the TT, Oliver's Mount and some of the many places we'd visited over the previous couple of months.

I put this down to being inspired during my return to the Isle of Man, our visit to the two bridges. That had kept me occupied. So much so that, now wait for it, you'd best be seated for this! I hadn't been in the Traf or the Corporation Club, any watering hole, in fact, since our 'Lady and Gentleman' shortly after I'd arrived back in Scarborough.

I know! What's that all about? Now let's be honest: the old, what is it John calls them? Ah yes! Gooey jiggery-pokery, butchers-esque plumbing, something like that. Well, those bits, they could do with a rest after all our galivanting and continental beer-fuelled escapades.

That was about to change. I'd been pacing back and forth at home for what seemed like hours, but was most likely closer to fifteen minutes, huffing and puffing like Winnie does when she wants to herd me upstairs for a dog nap. Evidently, Lisa was concerned about my shoe leather, the laminate flooring and her own mental health.

"Go on! Get Ut! Get Ut!" she'd said as she ushered

me through the front door and out into the street. "Go have a thimble, you could do with and know you want one." A very polite way of telling me to sling my hook, pronto.

No arguments from me.

"Say hello to Genge!" she called after me.

"If he's out!" I replied, not turning my head, avoiding the temptation to break into a sprint.

The 'Get ut?' Another of my made-up sayings, sorry. Although interestingly enough, to me that is. 'Ut' is Norwegian for exit, saw it on a travel vlog the other day. Quite appropriate then, good job it wasn't the Swedish version… 'Utfart'… That would have had the neighbours twitching at the drapes. And who could blame them as I utfarted all the way to the end of the street!

Aahhhh! Back in the local, the Traf. It was nice to be home, where everybody knows your name. Your real name. Time for a thimble or two, my codeword to Lisa when I require a few thinking pints, a time to reflect, alone.

"Pint please, Lynn."

"Well hello, stranger, where on earth have you been? Haven't seen you in ages! Been up to much?"

"Not a lot, Lynn, this and that."

"Nothing I wouldn't do, I hope! Keeping out of trouble?"

"Oh, for the most part." I grinned, winked.

And so, I stood at the corner of the bar, one part of my brain in reflection mode, thinking about my recent experiences, the ramifications of our defeat of the creature in the cave. Was I all-in now? Would my involvement come home to roost? Was I a bright light strobing on their radar screen? Or had the opposition been aware of my existence from day one? According to John, he wasn't the only one who'd been observing me over the years. The other side of my brain, chatting to Lynn, people at the bar, greeting newcomers and bidding farewell to those, whose thirsts quenched, were heading home, gone from each other's minds until next our paths crossed. This place, the pub, may as well have been a transit destination, a node accessed via portal. It felt like we faded away from people's consciousnesses as soon as we left the premises, made whole and real when we stepped over the threshold once more, unless we were gathered in that limbo realm, better known as the smoking area.

I shrugged off this melancholia before it took hold and dragged me down, swallowed me up, talking of which, "Another please, Lynn."

I was daydreaming, thinking about this, pondering that. The battery on my SV650 race bike, when would so and so arrive? Best chase it up. Ring them up? No, I hate talking on the phone. I'll email tomorrow. You know, organising my mental diary.

And then, John sidled up to me at the bar. I'd have toppled off my stool if I'd been sitting on one, startled as I was!

But seeing as I was in the standing position, a double-take sufficed.

Without any prompting, Lynn placed a pint of

Guinness before John, and I had to endure an agonising few seconds before I could begin my inevitable inquisition.

And so, I waited patiently, or my best attempt at, whilst he savoured the first few sips of that glorious dark liquid crowned with a creamy white top. Yes, I agree sounds like me and Mr Guinness need to get a room. It's just that I love that dark nectar, unfortunately it's a no go now, the feelings aren't mutual, high blood sugar, you see.

John tilted his head towards the quiet corner near the pub's kitchen. I dutifully followed, curious to hear what the score was. Okay, bursting at the seams to know what the hell was going on. I'd not expected to see my friend so soon.

John Willis was back at my Mum's, not just for a flying visit, here at least over the winter months. Like the cat that got the cream! He'd been spoilt rotten on his return, sworn my Mum to secrecy the better to avoid ruining the surprise.

"Well then, what was the point of my trip to the Isle of Man…"

I broke off, my bubble burst, by myself. I knew fine well why I'd gone there. It was my decision. My question was pointless, it had no bearing. I threw a few stalling words out there to give me time to process what I wanted to really ask, if anything.

"Hang on."

"Good game that was!" replied John Willis.

"Yes, oh yeah! No, wait!"

"I like it here, Whiskers, like your Mum."

"What's happening, what are you saying?"

"Ha! Ha! You're too easy, Whiskers. Your Mum isn't over the hill yet, you know. Seriously, I like her company, I like it here. Besides, I have a feeling our services will be called upon before too long, back in the fray."

"A feeling?"

"That's what I said. Besides…" he said, rubbing his hands together, "new season: Oliver's Mount. Where else would I be?"

"And what about the Isle of Man, your lodgings?"

"Oh, that's taken care of, the Stallards will welcome me back when I inevitably return. Besides, I pay a year in advance, saves messing about with standing orders and all that stuff. Anyway, I think your Mum appreciates the company, as do I."

"Are you lonely, John?"

"Lonely? How can I be? I've got you to look after, haven't I? No, seriously. Not in the slightest, loneliness is a state of mind, albeit it can affect a person physically. But I'm not alone, spiritually, I'm connected. My mind is capable of being in several places at once, at a push. It's like being physically present in a place imagined. Admittedly it can get a bit confusing. The ill-prepared can easily feel a tad discombobulated."

"Fancy word…"

"Just one of my favourites, I try to use it whenever possible, use it or lose it. And you, Whiskers?"

"What about me? Oh. Rarely. I did experience a form of loneliness during lockdown. I think there are different shades, flavours of loneliness. Mine wasn't brought about by the fact of being alone, a little isolated. It manifested due to being apart, my loved ones, separated by distance, just out of reach. I think that shade is akin to the feelings of loss, closely related to a sense of bereavement. Where you've had that companionship, but suddenly, it's taken away. Some confuse loneliness with boredom. Two separate states, not even distant cousins in my book. The former an emotion, the latter a simple lack of imagination."

"So that's a yes then?"

I laughed out loud, drawing a few quizzical glances from various points of the bar. Good old John! A second bout of melancholia avoided, nipped in the bud.

"Come on, Whiskers, let's blow this joint. We need to lift our spirits, or pints. Down the hatch!"

We drained our glasses, returned them to the bar, said our farewells and disappeared into the night.

"Let's go to yours and have one of those kitchen discos I've been hearing all about."

"Yowl!" I exclaimed.

John replied in the form of a 360-degree spin.

At a little after ten, yes, we are rock and roll party animals without comparison, John took his leave, politely refusing the offer to sleep at the end of the bed. He portalled home. I wondered once more if that personal transportation portal gizmo would ever be available to yours truly. Whatever, it was time to shut down the party and head upstairs.

"Goodnight, Lisa. Night, night, Winnie."

I said in my head, 'Goodnight, John-boy.' An image formed in my mind's eye. A cat, grinning, head tilted. 'Goodnight, Whiskers!'

•

John here. So, it was the end of the beginning to butcher a quote. I lay in the club room at Whisker's Mum's house, thinking out loud. Strange saying that, are you thinking or simply talking to yourself? Or both? Back to the thoughts in hand... in hand? Never mind...

Why do I do what I do? To altruistically aid the human race? To atone, get back into the good books? Because it keeps me occupied, amused? It's fun, a real buzz? Whatever the reason, bear in mind there are no selfless deeds. Why do entrepreneurs often evolve into philanthropists? Simple answer, boredom. Long winded answer? They have everything, anything their individual imaginations allow them to desire. They've achieved all they can in their chosen field. They're driven to compromise. They seek out and get their kicks from the happiness of others, like parents watching their children, wide-eyed, opening presents on Christmas morning. When you play a game, the game of life, unlock all the achievements, find all the goodies, best all your rivals, sit atop the leaderboard, the game is finished, completed. Start with a fresh character? Maybe, same scenario though. These aren't bad people, they've provided employment, filled a need, some service or product or whatever, and now they help people in a more charitable way, living vicariously through the eyes of others. It's a shame they still feel empty. Don't envy others, it's wasted energy, these few kingmakers, their metaphorical cup overflowed with all the 'stuff' we dream and strive for, but it's lonely at the top.

That word again, emotion in the words of Whiskers. Loneliness.

And the motto of the story? Well, there isn't one. If you could sum it up with a sentence, it wouldn't be much of a tale, would it?

Cheers.

John Willis

The End

EPILOGUE

Six months later, autumn was approaching in all its bronze leafed glory.

John portalled directly into our living room on Murchison Street. He didn't startle me. For one, I could sense the signature of his imminent arrival. Secondly, I wasn't in the living room, I was upstairs playing my latest game. I made my way downstairs, Winnie following closely in my wake.

"Trouble?"

"Let's call it a problem. I need, no, I require, access to that finely tuned brain of yours."

No sign of sarcasm, must be serious. Access? Sounded a bit messy, invasive.

As if sensing my concerns, he added, "In short, I need an opinion, from the human perspective. Grab your gear, Mr Whiskers, we've got work to do!"

A bit of a quandary! Should I stay, or should I go? I think we all know the answer to that!

THE REAL JOHN WILLIS

John Willis lives above the Trafalgar Pub in Scarborough. His human project, for cats really don't have owners, according to them, is Teigan Purvis.

When Teigan told me her cat went by the name John Willis, I thought it was great, funny, cool. Later that night, this story, the characters came to life in my mind. Next step, writing, and boy did it flow!

I'd like to take the credit, but how can a cat named JW not develop into a really interesting character and form the bed-rock of an entertaining tale? Hah! Tale, tail… apologies, shouldn't laugh at my own feeble attempts at humour!

Thanks once again for the literary inspiration, Teigan!

THE ARTWORK

The artwork that adorns both the front and rear cover of this book was painted by Pete Rumney. I commissioned Pete to produce for me an original piece of art. I provided him with a comprehensive brief and sent him various images: me seated on a bench in my Mum's garden, Teigan and Callum walking down the street. I channelled my inner David Bailey for that one.

Hari Burrows and Steve Morris sent me various images from Aberdare Park. These were taken during and in the days following the 2024 road races. I think it all came together really well: 'Teamwork makes the dream work!' as Daley Mathison used to say.

From my perspective, it sets the scene fantastically well. To pardon the pun, Pete most definitely knocked it out of the park!

www.peterumneyart.co.uk

THE JOEY DUNLOP FOUNDATION

As I did with my first book, I shall be donating 10% from every book sale to the Joey Dunlop Foundation.

The foundation is a charitable organisation, run by volunteers and based on the Isle of Man.

They provide accommodation at Bradden Bridge House for disabled visitors to the Isle.

Throughout the year, they are busy attending various motorcycle meetings and related events, in order to provide state-of-the-art facilities for their guests.

I was lucky enough to win a motorcycle in their annual raffle in 2020 and since that day I've vowed to support them to the best of my ability.

Find out more about their good works, facilities and history at: www.joeydunlopfoundation.com

Many thanks

Joel

REFERENCES

7 Days to Die - The Fun Pimps
Carl Jung
DayZ - Bohemia Interactive
Heart of Darkness - Joseph Conrad
Hercule Poirot - Agatha Christie
Iain M. Banks
John H. Glover-Kind - "I Do like to Be Beside the Seaside" – Song: 1907
John Le Carré
Peter F. Hamilton
Red Dwarf
Road Racing News
Smiley's People
The Hitchhiker's Guide to the Galaxy
David Knowles obituary – www.palatinate.org.uk/david-knowles-obituary-of-the-former-journalist-and-durham-alumnus/

ALSO BY THIS AUTHOR

DALEY MATHISON
FORGET ME NOT!

The Official Biography for Daley Mathison, written by Joel Neil Campbell and authorised by Daley's daughter; Daisy Blu Mathison.

Daley was young and handsome with a warm, friendly personality. Cheeky, charming and generous with his time. Added to these attributes was an abundance of talent in his given sport, the sport being, Motorcycle racing.

All the pieces were falling into place: married to Natalie in 2015 and the arrival of a daughter, Daisy Blu, in 2016. The first of three consecutive Isle of Man TT podiums followed shortly thereafter. The 2016 season also saw Daley retain his title as European MotoE Champion.

Within himself he had a burning desire, an ambition to take the next step, to become a full-time, professional Road Racer.

On the cusp of the realisation of his dream, it was cruelly taken away. Daley, an accomplished and experienced TT racer had an accident during the 2019 TT.

The dream would no longer be fulfilled.

Available in e-book format via the Amazon Kindle store.